· NO CHILDREN ·

· NO PETS ·

The entire Sanders family—Mother, Don, Jane, four-year-old Betsy, and Victoria the cat—inherited an apartment house in Palm Glade, Florida. Everyone looked forward to a rest, but they reckoned without the strange tenants at 303 Oleander Drive. Little did they dream that they would soon become involved not only with a hurricane, but also with Miss Gidding's carefully guarded secret, Mrs. Pennypacker's ruby clip, a missing superintendent, and a strange and homeless boy.

Marion Holland

NO CHILDREN
NO PETS

 Avyx

No Children, No Pets
Published 2012 by Avyx, Inc., Littleton, CO 80122

Original Copyright © 1956 Marion Holland
L.C. catalog card number: 56-8898
Originally published in 1956 by Alfred A. Knopf, Inc. Permission to reprint this book was
sought from Alfred A. Knopf, Inc. and all known subsidiaries and assigns. Current Copyright owner is unknown.

ISBN: 978-1-935570-10-3

www.avyx.com

Avyx, Inc.
8032 South Grant Way
Littleton, CO 80122
USA
303-483-0140

TO
the tenants of the
real apartment house in
Florida this story is
affectionately dedicated.

· CONTENTS ·

• NO CHILDREN •

• NO PETS •

Air Mail, Registered

JANE was alone in the house when the registered air mail letter came.

At least, she was alone if you didn't count four-year-old Betsy, who was taking a nap. Mother wouldn't be home from work for an hour yet, and Don had gone off to the playground pool to swim. It was so hot that Jane almost wished she had taken Betsy and gone, too. But no matter how cooled off you got in the pool, you always arrived home again hotter than ever, after the long walk through the crowded, stifling streets.

Victoria, the cat, had the right idea. She was stretched out, as flat as a gray fur rug, on the floor just inside the front screen door. When the doorbell rang, Victoria didn't even twitch a whisker, and Jane had to step over her to take the letter from the postman.

"Sign here," he said, handing her a slip of paper and a stubby pencil.

Jane stared at the thick envelope. "But it's not for me, it's for my mother."

"Sign her name, and your name under it."

Jane wrote *Mrs. Mary Sanders*, and underneath it, *Jane Anne Sanders*. The handwriting was a little wobbly because the paper was propped up against the door jamb, but the postman didn't even glance at it. He stuck the paper in a little notebook and walked off, whistling, just as though he took registered air mail letters to people every day of the week. Which perhaps he did.

Jane had seen that postmark before. Palm Glade, Florida. That was where Mother's great-uncle John lived. Every year they got a letter from him, at Christmas time, and every year it was the same thing.

Three one dollar bills, one each for Don and Jane
and Betsy, and a letter for Mother, full of good ad-
vice. Like "Waste not, want not," and "A penny
saved is a penny earned."

Mother only laughed at the letters and threw them
in the wastebasket, but they always made Jane and
Don mad. As if they ever wasted anything at the Sanders' house, especially since Father died and Mother
went back to her old job at the city library.

But this wasn't Christmas. It was the third of Au-
gust. Maybe Great-great-uncle John had decided to
send them an un-Christmas present for once. Not
that it would be a bit like him, thought Jane, prop-
ping the letter up on the bookcase where Mother
would be sure to see it the minute she came in.

But it was Don who came in first, carrying his wet
bathing trunks. "Boy, is it ever hot outside," he complained, stepping over Victoria. "You could fry an
egg on the pavement. Hey, where did that letter come
from? It wasn't in the mail this morning."

"It's for Mother," said Jane. "From Great-great-
uncle John."

"Bet it isn't," he retorted. "Look at the stamps.
Registered, thirty cents, air mail, six cents. Thirty-
six cents on a letter you could send for three! Waste
not, want not, you know."

"Well, put it down before you drip all over it," said Jane loftily. Even if Don was bigger than she was, she was more than a year older, and she didn't believe in letting him forget it. "Go hang your bathing trunks in the bathroom, and be quiet about it or you'll wake Bets," she added.

"She isn't asleep," called Don from the back of the house. "Anyway, she isn't in bed."

"She must have gone out back to play," said Jane, heading for the kitchen. The refrigerator door was open, and Jane shut it on the way by. She looked out in the tiny paved yard, just big enough for the trash cans and Betsy's little sand box.

"*Elizabeth Louisa Sanders!*" exclaimed Jane. "What are you doing?"

Betsy looked up with big solemn eyes. Her curls were pulled up on top of her head and fastened with a rubber band, on account of the heat, and her pink face was streaked with dirt and sweat. "It is not either hot enough to fry an egg," she said reproachfully.

The egg carton, which should have been in the refrigerator, was on the back step, and there were big globs of raw egg, mixed with shells, on the hot cement. The remains of at least three more eggs were dribbling down the front of Betsy's sunsuit.

"Oh, Bets!" wailed Jane. "Just look at the mess,

and Mother will be home any minute. And eggs cost money, too— And stop laughing!" she added angrily, to Don. "This is all your fault, going around all the time saying it's hot enough to fry an egg."

"But I didn't really mean it—"

"You can just quit grinning and clean up this mess while I wash Bets, and I do really mean it," said Jane grimly.

She stripped off Betsy's sunsuit and tossed it in

"It is not either hot enough to fry an egg."

the sink. She pulled her hand back from the hot water faucet and turned on the cold, instead; hot water would only cook the eggs into the cloth. She left the sunsuit soaking and started water running in the bathtub and dumped Betsy in.

"Ugh, there's even egg in your hair," exclaimed Jane. "I'll have to shampoo you." The rubber band snarled in Betsy's curls as Jane pulled it off, and Betsy clutched at her head and howled. She squinched her eyes tight shut and went right on howling as Jane tipped her back in the water, lathered her hair, and then rinsed out the suds.

"You can stop yelling now," said Jane finally. She rubbed Betsy's hair with a towel and asked: "Soap in your eyes?"

Betsy opened her eyes cautiously. "No," she said in a surprised voice. "But there's soap in my mouth," she added indignantly.

"Next time, keep it shut," said Jane unsympathetically. She put a clean sunsuit on Betsy and sat her down on the living room floor with a box of crayons and a coloring book. "And stay there," she said fiercely, "until Mother gets home."

Don was scraping the remains of the last egg onto a piece of cardboard. He dumped it into the garbage can and called in to Jane: "Were there any eggs left?"

"One. Why?"

"Well, Betsy's right, it isn't hot enough to fry an egg on the pavement. But you know something? If I had some grease to keep it from sticking, I bet you I could fry an egg on the lid of the garbage can. It's twice as hot as the pavement."

Before Jane could say what she thought of *that* idea, she heard Mother at the front door. "Mother!" she called. "A letter for you! Registered air mail!"

Mother was carrying a sack of groceries in her arms, so she didn't see Victoria on the floor. Victoria let out an indignant yowl when Mother stepped on her tail, and leaped onto the bookcase, knocking the letter to the floor.

"Oh, Mother," wailed Betsy. "You stepped on her *tail!*"

Jane snatched the letter up and waved it at Mother. "Open it, open it!" she urged.

"Poor Victoria," crooned Betsy, hauling the cat off the bookcase. "You ought to say, 'I'm sorry, Victoria.'"

"I'm sorry, Victoria. She always gets stepped on when she lies in the doorway and she knows it. Don! Come and take the groceries."

Don carried the bag into the kitchen, shouting over his shoulder: "Did you see your letter, with thirty-six cents worth of stamps on it? Hadn't you better open it right away?"

Mother took off her hat and pushed her damp hair back from her forehead; then she sat down and kicked off her shoes. Then she took the letter from Jane and fanned her face with it before she opened it. While Mother read the typewritten letter, Jane picked up the envelope and shook it, but no dollar bills fell out. Not that she had expected them to, really.

"Is it from Great-great-uncle John?" she asked.

"No. It's from a lawyer."

"I told you so," said Don.

"But it's about Great-uncle John. He's dead."

"Oh," said Jane, and stopped, embarrassed. She felt as though she ought to say something more. That she was sorry, or something. But after all, she had never even seen Great-great-uncle John.

Betsy knew what to say. She looked up from the cat on her lap and remarked politely: "I hope he had a lovely funeral. Like my goldfish."

"But it wouldn't take pages and pages, just to say that," said Don hopefully. "Maybe he's left us a million dollars."

"No, he didn't leave us any money," said Mother, glancing back over the letter.

"Not even a thousand? Not even a hundred?" asked Don. "Not even *anything?*"

"He did leave us something. An apartment house in Palm Glade. I believe it was where he lived himself."

"Oh, Mother, is it near the ocean?" cried Jane. "Oh, I hope it's near the ocean. Why can't we just go and live in it? Think of the money you'd save, not paying any rent!"

"Hot diggity, a whole apartment house!" shouted Don. "We can live in one apartment until all the dishes are dirty and everything is good and messed up, and then we can lock the door and move into the next apartment until all the dishes—"

"Oh, hush, Don," interrupted Jane. "No fooling, Mother, what are you going to do with it?"

"I don't know," replied Mother, looking a little dazed. "Sell it, I suppose. Mr. Merrill, he's the lawyer who is handling Great-uncle John's estate, writes that the place is in rather poor repair, but several people have already asked him whether it will be for sale. And there's a lot in the letter about taxes that I don't understand very clearly. Oh dear, he seems to think that I ought to go down and take a look at the place before I make up my mind about it."

"Oh, *let's!*" cried Jane. "Why, I've never been farther away from Philadelphia than Baltimore in my whole life. Just think, *Florida!* We studied about it in school—palm trees, flamingos, orange groves—"

"Sharks, alligators, hurricanes," added Don. "We studied about it, too."

"Oh, dear, I just don't know," murmured Mother, frowning at the letter. "Of course, I would have to take the lot of you, and it would be rather expensive. Still, I suppose I'll get some money out of it, eventually, and it's not as if you'd be missing any school. And luckily I have two weeks' vacation coming to me."

"And luckily I won't be twelve until October so I can still go half-fare, and luckily Betsy is only four so she can go for free," said Don practically.

"And luckily Victoria is only a cat so she can go in a box," added Jane.

"Oh, no. We couldn't possibly take Victoria with us!" exclaimed Mother.

Betsy clutched Victoria fiercely. "Yes, we can too take Victoria!" she cried.

"But we're going on a long trip, on a train, and Victoria would hate it," explained Mother. "Perhaps the Schmidts will feed her while we're gone."

The Schmidts lived over them, in the upstairs half

of the little row house. "They're going away on their vacation tomorrow," objected Jane. "For two whole weeks. Ellen was telling me yesterday."

"I just love riding on trains," announced Betsy dreamily.

"Why, you've never been on a train in your whole life!" exclaimed Don.

"You don't know *everything* about me," replied Betsy coldly. "You think you do, but you don't. And Victoria just loves riding on trains, too."

"That cat," said Mother.

So, in the end, they took Victoria. Mother arranged with the library to take her two weeks' vacation now, and more time if she needed it; and Victoria travelled in a box with a screened lid and behaved very well, considering.

They went in the coach train, the kind where the passengers are supposed to sleep sitting up, because Mother couldn't afford a Pullman, even if she had just inherited an apartment house in Florida. Nobody slept very well, and by the time they got off in Palm Glade, late in the afternoon, they were stiff and tired and rumpled.

They were the only passengers for Palm Glade. There wasn't a living thing in sight, except for a dog asleep in the shadow of a baggage truck, and the station master half-asleep in his little office. He roused himself enough to say that no taxis met the trains in the summer, but that he could give them directions to 303 Oleander Drive, if they wanted to walk.

So they walked. Mother carried one suitcase, and Jane and Don took turns carrying the other suitcase and Victoria's box.

Betsy lagged far behind. "I'm so hot," she complained.

"But it's nice clean heat," said Jane comfortingly. "It doesn't smell of trucks and melted asphalt, the way it does at home. It smells of sand and flowers and —and—" She sniffed. "It smells of ocean! It really does. Oh, Mother, the ocean can't be so very far away if we can smell it!"

"How do you know what an ocean smells like?" argued Don. "You never smelled one before."

"I just know," replied Jane. "Come on, Betsy, I'll take your hand."

Palm Glade was bigger than it looked from the station. They walked along the main street for three or four blocks. More than half the little stores had signs saying *Will Reopen November 15*, or *Closed for the Summer*. There were vacant lots, too, full of brightly colored flowers growing wild, right there be-

Betsy lagged far behind.

side the sidewalk. Then they found the right corner
and turned onto Oleander Drive.

There were no sidewalks on Oleander Drive, so
they walked in the pebbly, sandy street. They passed
several apartment houses, and a big hotel, boarded up.

Betsy began to limp. "Aren't we there yet?" she
whimpered. "There's a stone in my shoe."

"Just a little farther," said Jane cheerfully, hoping
she was right. And she was. There it was, number
303. They set their luggage down and stared at their
new property.

It was a long, low, white stucco building with a
red tile roof. Masses of shrubbery, covered with
strange brilliant flowers, grew all around it. There
were several different kinds of palm trees on the wide
green lawn, and one enormous live oak with a cluster
of garden chairs beneath it. An elderly lady was sitting in one of the chairs, knitting and reading, both
at once. She glanced up and peered at them over
her glasses and then went back to her knitting and
reading.

Somehow it hadn't occurred to Jane until this very
minute that there would actually be people living
here, and she suddenly felt very dusty and bedraggled. She straightened Betsy's hair ribbon and tried
to smooth down her own rumpled dress.

Don was reading out loud the little signs beside the front door:

NO PEDDLERS.

NO CHILDREN. NO PETS.

MANAGER, AP'T 5.

"Thank goodness there's a manager," said Mother. "Let's go find apartment five."

They picked up their luggage and straggled into the building. The long hall was barely lighted by two feeble bulbs, and it was all they could do to make out the numbers on the doors.

"Remind me to put in some stronger light bulbs tomorrow," said Mother.

"A penny saved is a penny earned," quoted Don. He caught Jane's eye and they both grinned.

Apartment five turned out to be at the far end of the long dim hall. Mother set down her suitcase and knocked on the door.

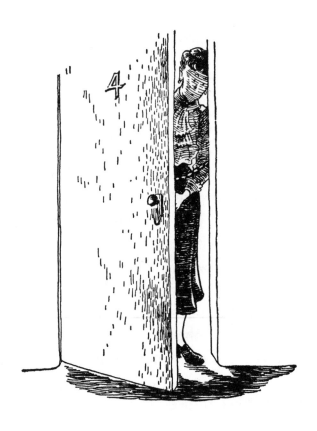

303 Oleander Drive

🏴 JANE shifted her suitcase from her right hand to her left and waggled her fingers to get the numbness out of them. She looked down the long hall at ten closed doors, five on each side.

Betsy pulled at Jane's skirt. "I have to take my shoes off," she whispered urgently.

"Not yet," Jane whispered back. "Pretty soon."

Mother knocked at the door of number five again, but there was still no answer. "There must be somebody home, somewhere," she said, and walked back to the next door, number four, and knocked on it.

They heard footsteps on the other side of the door; then the lock clicked and the door opened about two inches. "No peddlers," said a small thin voice. The door shut and the lock clicked again.

Mother knocked again, loudly. Again the door opened a crack, and Mother said quickly: "I am not selling anything. Can you tell me where to find the manager?"

The door opened wider, wide enough for Jane to see a chain across the opening; a small scared-looking lady peered out past Mother at Jane and Don and Betsy. "If you want to see about renting an apartment, I am afraid you are wasting your time," she said. "No children. There is a sign out front."

She started to close the door again, but this time Mother had her foot in it. "I don't want to see about renting an apartment," said Mother in an exasperated voice. "And I do want to see the manager. I am Mrs. Sanders, the new owner of this building."

"Oh my goodness! I mean, how do you do? I am Miss Giddings, Lucy Giddings." Miss Giddings extended a pale thin hand past the chain, and Mother solemnly shook it.

"How do you do?" said Mother. "I hate to bother you, so if you will just tell me where to find the manager—?"

"The manager?" squeaked Miss Giddings. "Dear me, it never rains but it pours, doesn't it? I mean, I am afraid you can't find the manager, but Mrs. Pennypacker has his keys, so if you will just come with me—"

Miss Giddings unfastened the chain, slipped out, and closed the door quickly behind her. "Mrs. Pennypacker," she went on, as she led the way down the hall, "is the only tenant in this building who has lived here longer than I have. *I* have made this my home for seventeen years, and I do hope, Mrs. Sanders—we *all* hope—that you are not planning any changes. Here we are."

She stopped in front of apartment number one and tapped lightly on the door. "About the keys," she went on earnestly, "the manager really left them in my care, but Myrtle Pennypacker is so efficient, so very, very efficient, that she thought— Dear me, perhaps she isn't home."

"Perhaps she didn't hear you," said Mother, and knocked loudly on the door.

The door flew open at once. Mrs. Pennypacker was a large, commanding lady in a purple-flowered dress. Her eyes, behind glittering pinch-on glasses, swept over the Sanders family and their shabby luggage, but she addressed herself to Miss Giddings.

"Really, Lucy!" she exclaimed in a booming voice. "No need to batter the door down. I heard you the first time."

"It will only take a minute," apologized Miss Giddings. "This is Mrs. Sanders, Myrtle. Mrs. Sanders would like to have the keys."

"The *keys!*" exclaimed Mrs. Pennypacker. "Lucy Giddings, are you out of your mind?"

"I am the new owner of this building," said Mother, rather sharply. "Mr. McGregor was my great-uncle, and he left it to me in his will."

"Well, really. How do you do? I am afraid that we are rather upset around here. So many things, all at once. Poor Mr. McGregor passing away, and then that unreliable manager disappearing. Now a new owner. Most upsetting. But of course, you want the keys. Won't you step in a moment?"

Jane couldn't decide whether Mrs. Pennypacker meant them all to step in, or just Mother; but Betsy followed Mother in, so Jane went in, too, to keep an eye on Betsy. Miss Giddings fluttered in after her, and Don stood uncomfortably, just inside the doorway, still holding Victoria's box.

"I will get the keys. Please be seated," said Mrs. Pennypacker with a wave of her hand, and swept out of the room.

The room was a large one, but so full of chairs and sofas and little tables and fern stands that there was hardly space to move without bumping into something. Jane picked out a wide chair and sat down, pulling Betsy down beside her.

Betsy promptly unbuckled one sandal and took it off, shaking a pile of sand and pebbles onto the rug. "Oh, Bets, not yet!" whispered Jane. "Put it back on. Quick!"

Instead, Betsy removed the other sandal and shook the sand out of it. Jane quickly set her own two feet down over the scrunchy sandy place, and just in time, as Mrs. Pennypacker returned, jangling a large bunch of keys.

"These two big ones are the front door and the back door of the building," she said to Mother. "The two little ones are the storage closet and the meter room. The others are the doors to the apartments. Each has its proper number on it. Of course, you will not have to use them, except in an emergency, as all the apartments are occupied."

"All of them?" asked Mother in dismay. "I was counting on staying here until I can get this business settled."

"With these *children?*" Mrs. Pennypacker raised her eyebrows so suddenly that her glasses popped off the bridge of her nose and she caught them as they fell.

"Now, Myrtle, number six is vacant," put in Miss Giddings anxiously. "Your poor dear uncle lived in number six," she explained to Mother. "And the manager's apartment, too. Temporarily."

"Temporarily!" snorted Mrs. Pennypacker. "You mark my words, Lucy Giddings, we have seen the last of *him.* However, five and six are the two smallest apartments in the building, and with such a large family, Mrs. Sanders, I am sure you would be more comfortable elsewhere."

Jane got so interested, listening to all this, that she let Betsy stand up and walk away. Betsy drifted around the room on silent sock feet, in and out among the tables and chairs, until she came to Victoria's box. She squatted down and unlatched the lid and lifted Victoria out.

Victoria had put in an unsettling night and day;

she scratched Betsy on the wrist, and Betsy dropped her with a wail. Don made a grab, but Victoria dodged him and raced across the room.

"*Cats!*" exclaimed Mrs. Pennypacker in a horrified voice.

Betsy opened her mouth wide and howled: "I hate this awful old place. I want to go home!"

"*Children!*" exclaimed Mrs. Pennypacker, in the same horrified voice.

Mother picked Betsy up and tried to comfort her, but Betsy refused to be comforted. "And I hate these awful old *people!*" she roared.

Jane and Don stalked Victoria around the furniture. They cornered her under a chair and Jane reached down to pick her up, murmuring soothingly: "Come on, kitty, it's all right, kitty—"

Just then Mrs. Pennypacker charged down upon them, flapping her skirts and shouting: "Shoo! Scat! Get that animal out of here!"

Victoria shot out from under the chair and leaped onto the back of the sofa, her claws making a tearing sound in the shiny upholstery. She dodged Mother's outstretched hand and took off through the open door into the hallway.

Jane and Don ran after her, calling: "Kitty, kitty, kitty—" Betsy broke away from Mother and followed them, screaming at the top of her voice: "Catch her! Catch her!"

Mother ran after Betsy, and Miss Giddings darted out after Mother, wringing her hands and murmuring: "Oh my goodness, oh my goodness!"

Mrs. Pennypacker stood guard over her own doorway, flapping her skirts and shouting: "Scat!"

Victoria raced the length of the hall and doubled

Don made a grab.

back, with Don and Jane in hot pursuit. The noise of
shouting, screaming, and thudding feet filled the
narrow hallway. Doors popped open up and down the
hall, as tenants put their heads out to see what was
going on. Most of them hastily closed their doors
again, but one plump little woman dashed out with
a broom and began to wave it helpfully around.

"Please stand still, everybody!" implored Jane.
"You're only scaring her."

Nobody paid the slightest attention.

"Scat!" shouted Mrs. Pennypacker.

"Catch her! Catch her!" shrieked Betsy.

"Betsy, come here," commanded Mother.

"Look out, here she comes again!" gasped the
woman with the broom, making a wild swipe that
missed Victoria by three feet but only missed Miss
Giddings by about three inches.

Victoria cowered against a closed door halfway
down the hall. "Keep back, everybody. I've got her,"
panted Don, stooping down.

Then the door behind Victoria opened, and she
shot in through it. Don tumbled in after her, almost
upsetting the little man who had opened the door.

"Oh, Professor Quincy, do be careful!" implored
Miss Giddings.

Professor Quincy, a gnome-like little fellow with

a gleaming bald head and a small tidy beard, took in the situation at a glance. He stepped quietly back in and closed the door.

Behind the closed door there was silence for a moment, then a loud crash and the sound of running feet. Then silence again. Then Professor Quincy put his head out and announced solemnly: "The cat is caught. May I suggest that you all retire to a safe distance?"

Mother got a firm grip on Betsy. The woman with the broom went back into her apartment and shut the door. Miss Giddings retreated to the far end of the hall.

Don came out, carrying Victoria. Just at that moment, the lady who had been reading and knitting on the lawn opened the front screen door and stood there, staring.

"Shut that door!" bellowed Don, as Victoria dug her claws into him; but it was too late. Victoria struggled loose and simply streaked through that open door to freedom. Don pelted after her, brushing roughly against the woman, who was still standing there, holding the door.

"Myrtle!" exclaimed the woman. "Who are these people?"

"The new owners," replied Mrs. Pennypacker.

"Merciful heavens!" gasped the woman. She bundled her knitting under her arm, scuttled into the apartment next to Mrs. Pennypacker's, and slammed the door.

Oh, poor Victoria, thought Jane. We'll never catch her now, scared and lost in such a strange place— But just then Don opened the front door and held it to let a boy walk through, a boy a little bigger than Don, wearing faded blue jeans and carrying Victoria.

"He caught her!" cried Don triumphantly. "He was just coming up the walk, and he just reached down, and zingo, he had her."

"I'll take her," offered Jane. "She's scratching you something fierce."

"I don't know if I can pry her loose," said the boy. "Where do you want her put?"

"In here," called Mother from the doorway of number five. "And bring the luggage."

It was quite a procession down the corridor, the boy with Victoria, Jane with a suitcase, and Don with the other suitcase and Victoria's box, which Mrs. Pennypacker had set outside her door. Mother closed the door of number five behind them and breathed a loud sigh of relief.

Victoria leaped to the floor, spitting and growling, and flattened herself under a sagging sofa. Miss Giddings was tiptoing around the room, making little patting motions at the furniture and talking steadily at Mother.

"Of course, this apartment isn't furnished as nicely as some; Mr. McGregor thought that as it was just for the manager's use— But you will find everything you need, I hope— The kitchen is through here, and this is the door to a small bedroom, and then of course there is the sofa— But if you find you need more room, your late uncle's apartment is just across the hall and, of course, you have the keys—"

Mother sank onto the sofa. "Mercy, what a day," she groaned. "Won't you sit down, Miss Giddings? I'm afraid that right now I'm completely confused. Tell me, what is all this about a manager who is supposed to live here?"

Miss Giddings perched on the edge of a chair. "Mr. Brundage, you mean. The thing is that he has only been here a few weeks, so nobody really *knows* anything about him. The late Mr. McGregor always managed the building himself, right up until his last illness— A very thrifty man—"

"Waste not, want not?" suggested Don.

Mother frowned and shook her head at him, but Miss Giddings said eagerly: "Exactly. His very words. Then it got too much for him and he hired this Mr.

Brundage, such a *nice* young man, I thought, although Myrtle Pennypacker said— But I'm sure I hope and trust that it will turn out that Myrtle was wrong—"

Mother interrupted: "Please, just tell me one thing. Where is this Mr. Brundage?"

"But that's just it. Nobody *knows*," explained Miss Giddings. "He was here this morning, because he took Myrtle's kitchen screen to mend. Then, when I went to get my mail, the keys were in my mail box, along with a note, saying he had been called out of town on urgent personal business, and asking me to take charge of the keys— But, of course, Myrtle thought that *she* had better— Not that it matters, because now, of course, you have them—"

"Thank you very much," said Mother, standing up briskly. "I'm certainly not going to worry about it now, with all these hungry, tired children on my hands. I see that there are some cans and things in the kitchen."

"I'm sure it will be all right if you use what you need," said Miss Giddings, following Mother into the kitchen. Jane could hear her opening and shutting drawers.

"Whew!" exclaimed Jane. "Thanks anyway for catching our cat— Why, where did that boy go?"

"Out," said Don. "And I don't blame him. I bet he thinks everybody around here is stark raving mad."

"No wonder," said Jane. "Ooh, I'm so tired and sleepy it hurts."

Miss Giddings finally left; and Jane and Don helped Mother open cans and set the little table in the kitchen. Nobody had even missed Betsy when the door banged open and Mrs. Pennypacker marched in, dragging Betsy by the wrist.

"I found this child in my apartment," announced Mrs. Pennypacker. "Goodness knows how long she had been there before I noticed her."

"I had to get my shoes," said Betsy, in a small voice. She held out her scuffed sandals.

"Just walked in, without a by-your-leave," continued Mrs. Pennypacker. "Never even knocked."

"Come here, Betsy," said Mother gently. "You must always knock on a door and wait for someone to say *Come in*. You're big enough to know that."

"Twenty years," stated Mrs. Pennypacker. "Twenty years I have lived here, and in all that time there has never been a child in this building. Never."

From the safety of Mother's skirt, Betsy interrupted in a loud voice: "You just walked right in *here*."

"Betsy!" exclaimed Mother.

"Well, she did, and nobody said, Come in. And she's *plenty* big enough to know better."

Mrs. Pennypacker's face turned a dark red. "Well, really," she spluttered. "If your poor dear uncle had lived to see the day!" And she turned on her heel and walked out.

They had a strange meal of canned chicken noodle soup and canned peaches and crackers; and right in the middle of it, Betsy fell asleep with her head on the table. Mother carried her into the bedroom and tucked her in.

While Mother unpacked, Jane and Don did the dishes. Victoria finally emerged from under the sofa and rubbed around their ankles, purring demurely and acting like a perfect lady.

"You awful cat," said Jane, feeding her the soup Betsy hadn't finished. "And I never even got a chance to thank that boy for catching her. Did you?" she asked Don.

"Who, me? I wasn't even looking when he ducked out. But we'll probably see him around. He must live near here. I hope he does, anyway, because everyone else is sure about a hundred and ten years old."

Mother unlocked the apartment across the hall and fixed up Great-great-uncle John's bed for Jane, and

Mrs. Pennypacker marched in, dragging Betsy.

his living room couch for Don. Stretched out comfortably in bed, Jane tried to think back as far as morning, when they had pressed their noses against the train windows in Jacksonville and taken their first look at Florida. It seemed a million years ago, so much had happened since, and so fast. And most of it so perfectly awful.

"We only just got here, and everybody's mad at us already," she said, out loud. "I don't think I'm going to like it here."

"Huh?" mumbled Don from the next room.

"Nothing. Look, where do you think that Mr. Brundage went to?"

"How would I know?"

Jane thought of something else. "What did you break in that man's apartment? We heard the biggest crash."

"Oh, that. Victoria knocked the glass cover off a case full of shells."

"Shells? What kind of shells?"

"Just shells. Sea shells. He has 'em all over the place. Must collect 'em or something."

"Was he mad?"

"Not specially," mumbled Don. "Listen, quit talking, can't you? I'm going to sleep."

"I'll talk all I want to," snapped Jane. But while she was trying to think what to say next, she went to sleep.

An Ocean

WHEN Jane woke up in the morning, bright yellow sunlight was streaming across the bed, and the strangest noise was coming in the window. Clickety-clickety-*click*. Over and over again, exactly like somebody running a stick back and forth across a picket fence. But Jane couldn't remember seeing any picket fences yesterday. Or any people that looked as if they might run a stick across one, either.

She sat up and looked out the window. Right outside there was a tall, curved coconut palm; one enormous frond hung down across the window, and little gusts of wind were running down its stiff green fingers, clickety-*click*. Clickety-clickety-clickety-*click*. And the top of a thick bush was crowding up against the screen, simply covered with big pink flowers, all blooming away as if it was no trouble at all.

Jane jumped out of bed and pawed through the suitcase on the floor until she found shorts, an old shirt, and a pair of sneakers. When she was dressed, she opened the apartment door a cautious crack and peeked out. Way down at the end of the long hall, she could see sunlight through the front screen door, the door Victoria had tried to escape through. And there was another open door at this end of the hall, the back door, it must be, because through the screen she could see trash cans and clotheslines and a sort of shed.

And in between were all those other doors. All shut now, thank goodness. Quickly she stepped across the hall to number five and slipped in.

Mother was all dressed to go out. "I have an appointment with Mr. Merrill at nine," she explained.

"Keep an eye on Betsy and don't let her bother anybody. I'll get some real groceries on my way back."

Don was eating two bananas at once, one in each hand. "Have a banana," he said, with his mouth full. "Unless you'd rather have sardines or canned beans. That's all there is."

One good thing about nothing but bananas for breakfast is no dishes to wash. Jane tossed the empty peels into the garbage container and fed Victoria sardines right out of the can.

"Not that she deserves them, after the awful way she acted yesterday," said Jane. "Goodness, wouldn't it be embarrassing if that Mr. Brundage were to walk in and catch us feeding his sardines to our cat!"

"He might," said Don. "He sure expected to come back when he left."

"How do you know?"

"He left some of his stuff here. A suit and a raincoat and some shirts and socks."

"Donald Sanders! Does Mother know you've been prying around in somebody else's belongings?" demanded Jane.

"For Pete's sake, we're going to unpack and stay here a while, aren't we? And how are we going to do that if we don't open the closets and bureau drawers, just tell me that!" exclaimed Don.

"Victoria wants out," said Betsy.

"Oh, dear, now I'll have to go out with her and make sure she doesn't run away again," said Jane. "Of course, she's had a couple of meals here now, so maybe she's beginning to feel at home."

Jane shooed Betsy out the back door, and held the screen open for Victoria. Victoria did indeed feel at home; she paused on the doorsill, just the way she always did at home, neither out nor in, and refused to budge until Jane gave her a good shove. Then she walked haughtily around the trash cans and disappeared under a bush, the same pink-flowered bush Jane had noticed through her window. It was one of a row that stretched clear around the building, each one full to bursting with different colored flowers. Pink and white, orange and red, salmon and yellow.

"Ooh, pretty!" cried Betsy, reaching out a hand.

"Don't touch!" said Jane sharply. Then she thought, for goodness sakes, why not? "Go ahead, honey, pick a couple," she said. "I forgot, they're our own flowers."

Betsy ran from bush to bush, overwhelmed by so large a choice. At last she picked a red one and a pink one, and Jane tucked them into the barette that held her curls back.

"I can't see them," complained Betsy.

"But everybody else can," said Jane. "You look perfectly lovely."

Two of the tenants were sitting in the lawn chairs under the big tree, watching Jane and Betsy. When Jane glanced up at them, they put their heads close together and began talking. About us, I suppose, thought Jane. Don't they have anything better to do? "Come on, Bets," she whispered. "Let's go around on the other side of the building and see what it's like there."

On that side there was no lawn, just a thicket, almost a jungle of unpruned bushes, overgrown with vines that wound up the palm trees. It reminded Jane of a movie she had seen at school when they were studying Brazil. Up the Amazon in technicolor, she thought, and me right in the middle of it.

Miss Giddings came around the corner, carrying a watering can. Betsy ran up to her, shouting: "See my roses! I look perfectly lovely."

Miss Giddings nodded vaguely. "Not roses, child," she murmured. "Hibiscuses."

"Biscuits?" repeated Betsy in amazement.

Miss Giddings carried the watering can over to a cement bird bath, half hidden in trailing vines, and began to fill it. "I always do this, every morning," she explained earnestly. "I can't tell you how much the birdies appreciate it. Too many people neglect to put out fresh water for our little feathered friends," she went on, looking straight at Jane, as though Jane were one of these neglectful people. "Just because the ocean is so near, they seem to feel there is enough. But, of course, the ocean is no good, being salt."

"Which way is the ocean?" asked Jane.

Miss Giddings gestured with one hand.

"How far away is it?" asked Jane.

Miss Giddings didn't answer. She pulled a little box from a pocket and began scattering raisins on the ground, making soft little clucking noises and peering up at the tree tops. A mocking bird appeared on a vine leaf. Jane and Betsy stood perfectly still, as the mocker fluttered to the ground and began pecking up raisins at Miss Giddings's feet.

Something made Jane turn her head. Victoria was creeping silently from under a bush, belly flat, only the tip of her tail twitching ever so slightly.

"Scat!" hissed Jane.

The bird flashed up onto a palm frond. Victoria shot up the curved trunk after it. Halfway up, she paused, a spray of vine leaves draped coquettishly around her neck and her claws slipping in the smooth

bark. Then she slithered backwards down to the
ground and walked sedately off.

"Oh, I'm dreadfully sorry!" cried Jane. "I'll shut
Victoria up inside, if you'd like," she offered.

Miss Giddings did not even glance at her. "That
dreadful, *murdering* cat!" she exclaimed shrilly.
"Well then, the birds sha'n't come here any more."
She set the box of raisins down and marched over to
the bird bath and began tipping the water out of it.

Jane watched her struggling with the heavy bird
bath and wondered whether she ought to offer to help.
Then she noticed Betsy stuffing the last of Miss Giddings's raisins into her mouth; so she quickly took
Betsy by the wrist and towed her out to the street in
front of the building. Out of the corner of her eye,
she could see that there were now four chair-sitters
on the lawn; she just looked straight in front of her
and led Betsy up to the end of the block.

At the corner, she slowed down and let go of
Betsy's wrist. "We're going to take a nice walk and
find an ocean," she announced.

"What's a notion?" asked Betsy.

"An ocean. You'll see," promised Jane.

Back on the main street, she turned in the direction Miss Giddings had pointed, the opposite direc-

tion from the railroad station. They soon left the town behind, and the paved street turned into a sandy road, and the sun beat down on their heads. They walked and walked.

"Are you sure there's an ocean on this street?" asked Betsy finally. "Maybe we passed it already."

"You can't pass an ocean without noticing it," said Jane.

Suddenly the road ran up a little ridge all covered with tall coarse grass. At the top, a cool breeze hit them in the face, and—there was the ocean! They just stood and looked and looked.

"Oh, Jane," said Betsy at last, with a sigh, "it's so big."

It was, too. It was blue and sparkling, and it stretched out and out, to the very edge of the sky, and the white beach curved along beside it, on and on, to the very edge of the world. Half a dozen little sun-faded cottages were scattered along the sandy ridge above the beach, but they were all boarded up and empty. Jane and Betsy had all that wide water and sand and sky and sun all to themselves.

They ran across the hot white beach and took off their shoes at the very edge, where the little waves hissed up and darkened the sand. Jane waded and splashed and shouted; and the enormous empty spaces all around swallowed up the shouts, so they hardly made any noise at all.

Betsy cooled her bare feet in the foamy curved ruffles at the edge of the waves, but it was the sand she loved best. At home, sand cost money, and when the sand in her sand box got spilled out, she had to scrape it up and put it back in again, and it always had a dirty used look. But here, the whole world was made of glittering sand, as far as she could see, as deep as she could dig. She ran up and down the beach, screaming and laughing, kicking up great fountains of sand, scattering great handfuls of it, and still there was plenty more everywhere.

Finally she came panting back to Jane. "Let's live here forever and forever," she begged.

Jane sniffed the exciting smell from the ocean, and wiggled her toes deep into the damp sand, and she knew suddenly that there was nothing in the whole world she would like better than to live here forever and forever. There must be more to Palm Glade than apartments full of fussy old ladies; somewhere, there must be a school, and somewhere, houses with children living in them.

"Can we, Jane? Can we?" asked Betsy.

"I don't know," said Jane soberly. "Mother will

And—there was the ocean!

have to decide. Oh, Bets, there's sand in your hair and your ears and even your eyelashes. Stand still while I dust you off!"

They stayed until the sun was high in the sky and Betsy's nose was bright pink and her sunsuit pockets were bulging with bits of shiny broken shells she had picked out of the sand; then they put on their shoes and walked back to town. The walk back seemed much shorter, the way it always does.

Jane found a shortcut through an alley from the main street that took them right into the back yard and up to the back door without having to walk down Oleander Drive past the chair-sitters on the lawn. Mother had been shopping, and there was a fine big lunch waiting for them.

"We found an ocean!" announced Betsy importantly, as she sat down at the table. "All by ourselves we found one!"

"And it's not very far away, and it's wonderful! Oh, I wish we could—" Jane broke off and asked anxiously: "What does that lawyer think about the place? I mean, whether you ought to keep it or sell it? Did you talk to him about it?"

"Yes, I did," replied Mother. "And the way I feel now, I'm about ready to go straight home and let him sell it as soon as he can."

"But we just came," objected Don.

"Oh, Mother!" wailed Jane. "Go home, away from the ocean, and everything? Even if we can't stay and really live here, can't we just stay until school starts?"

"I don't really see how," replied Mother. "In the first place, there's a lot to do around a building like this. There's that enormous yard to take care of, and the trash and garbage to dispose of and the hall to keep clean, and I'm sure fuses are always burning out and little things like that."

"But maybe Mr. Brundage will be back in a day or so. He's supposed to do all those things, isn't he?" asked Jane hopefully.

"Even if he did, I don't see how I could pay him. There are taxes overdue on the place right now, and a huge assessment for paving the front street, which the town is going to do soon. Great-uncle John didn't set aside any money for these things, and apparently he hasn't spent a penny on the place in years. It looks pretty, with all the trees and flowers, but the paint is peeling off everywhere and the carpets are wearing thin, and most of the equipment in the apartments needs repairing or replacing."

"But why should we worry about that if the tenants don't?" asked Jane.

"The tenants *do*," replied Mother grimly. "There

has been a perfect parade of tenants through here, ever since I got back from Mr. Merrill's office, all complaining about leaky ceilings and dripping faucets and a dozen other things."

"It's a wonder they'd go on living here, if that's the way they feel about it," observed Jane, thinking to herself that it would be a big improvement if they all packed up and left.

"The rents are very reasonable, and most of the tenants have lived here a long time, and they're set in their ways," explained Mother. "Goodness knows there are plenty of fancy new places being built, all glass brick corners and picture windows, but somehow I don't think Great-uncle John's tenants would ever feel at home in them."

"What I can't understand," Don burst out, "is what he ever did with all his money, if he didn't even repair the roof over his own head!"

"Mr. Merrill told me that, too," said Mother. "It seems he'd been scraping together money for years, even including last month's rent money, and setting it aside for a trust fund for something to be called the John W. McGregor Humane Foundation. A sort of super-fancy home for stray dogs and cats, as nearly as I could figure out." She laughed. "I'm afraid it will never do any of us any good, but maybe Victoria can spend her declining years there."

"I wouldn't have thought he was all that fond of animals," marvelled Jane. "Look at the *No Pets* sign out front."

"I don't believe he was fond of animals at all. But he had no children or grandchildren, and I suppose he wanted to leave *something* behind with his name on it."

"Doggone, I wish he'd talked it over with me," grumbled Don. "For a million dollars I'd have changed *my* name to John W. McGregor, and then he could have left it all to me. For less than a million, even. And I'd have cut you all in on it, **too,**" he added generously.

Mike

❧ WHILE Mother put Betsy in bed for her nap, Jane and Don went out the back way to the tool shed.

"Boy, look at the junk!" said Don. "Nails, washers, wire, rope, rakes, barrels, flower pots, shutters, paint, putty— I bet he never threw anything away in his whole life! Waste not, want not."

Jane sat down on a coil of hose. "Shut up and listen to me," she said earnestly. "If Mother gets any more discouraged about this place, she's just going to take the next train home, and I don't want to go home. If you'd been to the ocean with me and Bets, you'd know why. So listen. Let's us do Mr. Brundage's work around here for a while, just until he gets back."

"I'm not so sure he's coming back," said Don.

"Why, you said he'd left some of his things."

"I know. But maybe he was just afraid to stick around long enough to pack," said Don. "You know Mrs. Pennypacker? Well, she was one of the ones that came in to see Mother while you were gone, and, boy, was she fit to be tied! Seems she's been checking over her belongings, because she never did trust Mr. Brundage, and now she claims a ruby and diamond clip of hers is missing, so naturally she thinks Mr. Brundage stole it and lammed, and she wants to notify the police and sue everybody in sight and I don't know what all. What's a clip, anyway?"

"Well, it's a sort of a—a— Oh, it's just a *thing*, something that ladies stick on their clothes when they want to look all dressed up. What makes her think Mr. Brundage stole it?"

"She says she wore it out to dinner day before yesterday, and took it off when she got back, but she

doesn't think she put it away. Just set it down somewhere. Well, then, next morning—yesterday, that
was—Mr. Brundage was in her apartment to get a
busted screen and the next thing anybody knew, he
was gone. So now she says she hasn't seen the ruby
clip since then, and not only is it very valuable, but
the ruby was out of her poor dear mother's engage-
ment ring, and she wouldn't take a million dollars
for it, and yaketty, yaketty, yak. No wonder Mother's
fed up."

"Oh, it'll turn up. Her apartment's so cluttered up
with stuff you could lose a St. Bernard in it, let alone
a ruby clip. Look here, you never answered me. Will
you help me keep the place tidied up and all? We
could work mornings and go swimming afternoons."

"Work? Some vacation."

"It's better than no vacation at all, and that's what
you'll get if Mother takes you straight home to Philadelphia."

"Well, O.K. Anyway, I already decided to stick
around and solve this mystery. Will Myrtle Pennypacker Recover the Missing Ruby? What was the
Urgent Message for the Vanishing Manager, or Has
he Simply Taken It on the Lam? Tune in tomorrow,
same time, same station. I'm going to do me some
sleuthing."

"You'll have to do it on your own time, then. You're going to work now," said Jane. "You might start on the lawn. It looks terrible."

"Must be a mower in here somewhere," said Don, picking his way to the back of the shed. "Yep, here it is and it's a gasoline job. Bet he bought it second-hand. Help me clear a path to get it out."

They piled things to one side. "Ugh, look at the musty old awnings," said Jane. "I ought to hang them on the line to air. And this must be Mrs. Pennypacker's screen, the one Mr. Brundage took to mend. I can do that while you mow the lawn."

Don pushed the mower out and studied it. "I've never run one of these things, but I've watched people do it. Lemme see. Connect the spark, push the choke over, wind up the rope—and yank!"

On the third yank, the motor caught with a roar. Don monkeyed around with the gears on the handle; the blades began whirring; the wheels started with a jerk; and Don clattered off across the back lawn in a shower of grass.

Jane found a pair of rusty shears and cut out a patch for the torn screen. Then she unravelled a length of screen wire and set to work sewing the patch on with it. By and by she noticed the noise of the mower had stopped and went to investigate.

Don and another boy were squatting beside the lawn mower. Why, it was the boy who had caught Victoria for them yesterday! "Hi!" shouted Jane. "I hope Don thanked you for catching our cat."

"Well, not yet," admitted Don. "Say, this thing just conked out on me. I sure hope I haven't busted something."

"Thanks an awful lot, anyway," Jane said to the boy. "We'd never have caught up with her, she was simply wild. She'd been on a train, in a box, and then all these people kept yelling and grabbing at her."

"Oh, that's all right," mumbled the boy. "She ran right into me, and I just picked her up." He frowned at the mower; then he unscrewed the cap to the gas tank and squinted in. "Out of gas," he said.

"Whee! That's a relief," said Don. "Say, my name's Don Sanders and this is my sister, Jane, and if you don't have a sister, you don't know how lucky you are."

This was supposed to be a joke, but the boy didn't smile. He had a thin, serious face, and he needed a haircut; his straight sandy hair kept flopping down into his eyes. "My name's Mike," he said briefly.

"Do you know, you're the very first person we've met in Florida," said Jane eagerly. "Not counting the

"Say, this thing just conked out on me."

tenants, of course, and they're too old to count."

"Must be a can of gasoline in the shed some-where," said Don. They all three went into the shed and got in each other's way looking through it.

"It's an awful mess in here," apologized Jane. "This place belonged to our great-great-uncle and he died and left it to our mother, and we only got here yesterday, so we don't know where anything is. There's supposed to be a man here to take care of things, but he's disappeared."

"Everything in here but the kitchen sink," grumbled Don, poking around in a dark corner. "Ouch! Here *is* the kitchen sink! I just banged my shin on it."

And there was a kitchen sink, with the enamel chipping off and gaping holes where the faucets should be.

"And here's a gasoline can," reported Jane. "Empty."

"I'll go get some," said Don. "There's a gas station back a couple of blocks on the main street. Is there any special kind of gas you use in these things?" he asked Mike.

"The straight kind. Uncolored, if you can get it. I'll come with you, if you'd like."

"You bet. Wait. I have to get some money from Mother."

"Don never ran one of these things before," explained Jane, "so it sure is lucky you happened to come along. At home, in Philadelphia, our front door's right on the sidewalk, and the back yard's cement. I bet you know all about gasoline mowers."

"I ought to, I've run 'em enough. Tractors, too," said Mike.

"Oh, I've always wanted to run a tractor. It looks like such fun, bouncing along on the little seat," said Jane.

"It is, at first, but after a while it's just another job," replied Mike, and went off with Don to get the gasoline.

Jane finished patching the screen. It was tedious work, bending the thin wire in and out to sew the patch on smoothly, and her fingers were sore and prickled before she was through, but it was a tidy job and she was proud of it. However, Mrs. Pennypacker never even said thank you. All the time Jane was fitting the screen into place, Mrs. Pennypacker was talking about how she really ought to have a whole new screen, and not only for the kitchen window, but for all the other windows, too.

Jane was glad to get out doors again, where Mike was watching Don finish up the back lawn. "Let me try it a while!" she shouted, over the noise of the mower.

"I can't hear you!" bellowed Don.

"Then turn it off!" yelled Jane.

Don threw the mower out of gear, and the blades and wheels stopped; but the motor racketed right on. "I don't know how!" he shouted finally.

Mike leaned over and did something, and the motor quit. "You can short out the spark, or disconnect it, or push the choke over and flood the engine," he explained.

"I want to run it a while," said Jane.

"Look, this is man's work," argued Don. "Why don't you run off somewhere and find something else to do?"

"Some man you turned out to be," said Jane scornfully. "Can't even stop the engine. What were you going to do—push it around all day until it ran out of gas?"

"Aw, let her have a turn," said Mike. "But we've got to move those chairs before we do the side lawn."

"We've got to get the people out of 'em first," observed Don.

They all looked at the chair-sitters. Now there were five of them, knitting and reading and talking. "That's Miss Giddings, and the one that let Victoria escape, and the one that waved the broom around," said Jane in a low voice. "I don't know who the other two are. And I don't especially want to go and ask 'em to move."

"Maybe if we just start mowing around and around the edge, they'll take the hint and go," suggested Don.

So they started mowing around the edge of the lawn; and as the rackety machine and flying grass closed in on them, the chair-sitters gathered up their magazines and books and knitting, and departed indoors. The boys moved the chairs back out of the way, leaving Jane to finish up the grass under the tree.

Suddenly she saw a magazine lying on the grass. She fumbled desperately with the gears, trying to remember which lever stopped the wheels, but the mower kept right on going. Then she tried to swerve aside. But it was just like riding a bicycle and trying to dodge a brick in the street; the harder she tried to turn aside, the more stubbornly the mower headed straight for the magazine. There was a rattling, tearing noise, and bits of shredded magazine flew out from under the machine.

"I told you this was man's work," yelled Don, grabbing the handle away from her.

There was nothing for it but to gather up the mangled remains and carry them around to the trash can. She was careful to pick up every tiny bit, so that nobody could tell a magazine had been run over. I hope whoever owned that was through with it, she thought glumly. All this work, just to keep the tenants happy; and now here was something else for them to complain about.

While the boys finished up the front lawn and put the mower away, Jane made an enormous pitcher of lemonade. They all three sat around in the tool shed and drank every drop of it.

"Boy, this managing an apartment house is hot work," grumbled Don, fishing the last piece of ice out of the pitcher and rubbing his face with it. "I don't think the tenants appreciate it, either. Did you notice 'em slamming the windows down while we were mowing near the building?"

"Yes, and Mrs. Pennypacker didn't even thank me for mending the screen," said Jane. "But, after all, we aren't really doing it for *them*. We're doing it for Mother, and because we don't want to go home right away."

"Didn't you say something about a man who was supposed to take care of the place?" asked Mike.

"Yes, a Mr. Brundage. But we've never even seen him. He up and left before we got here, and nobody knows where he went or when he'll be back," explained Jane. "It's sort of peculiar."

"I'll say it is!" cried Don enthusiastically. "It's a regular mystery, and I'm working on it. Look, I found this little blank notebook in the desk in number six, and I'm writing down clues in it."

Mike pushed his hair back out of his eyes and stared from Jane to Don. "What's so peculiar about it?" he asked.

"Well, this man disappears, leaving a bunch of his clothes behind, and saying he's been called out of town on urgent business. Then later, Mrs. Pennypacker—wait till you see *her!*—comes boiling around and claims she's missing a ruby clip, whatever *that* is. Anyway, it was her poor dear mother's, and worth pots of money, and she's really steamed up about it."

"Does she think Mr. Brundage stole—took it?" asked Mike.

"Boy, does she! And I guess he could, but so could

a lot of other people, because the screen was out of her kitchen window until Jane put it back a little while ago, and anybody could get in behind those bushes and reach right in the window. I know, because I tried."

"Don! You didn't!" exclaimed Jane.

"Sure I did. How you going to find out anything unless you try? I bet I could even climb in the window without anybody seeing me, on account of the bushes. I didn't try, though," he added hastily, to Jane. "And if you ask me, there's some pretty suspicious-looking characters living right in this building. Wouldn't hurt to keep an eye on all of 'em."

"Oh, Don!" cried Jane. "Imagine Miss Giddings, or any of them, shinnying in Mrs. Pennypacker's window! It's ridiculous. What I think is, that clip will turn up, right where Mrs. Pennypacker put it, and Mr. Brundage will walk in with some perfectly good reason for being away. It *is* funny, though, how nobody seems to know a single thing about him. Where he came from, or where he went, or anything. I guess Great-great-uncle John did, or he wouldn't have hired him."

"Well, it's too late to ask *him*," Don pointed out. "Mother even went through his papers, looking for any letters to Mr. Brundage, or from him, so as to find some address, but there wasn't a thing."

"Do you think Mr. Brundage took the ruby clip?" asked Mike.

Don scratched his head. "Well, you know how it is, the first one you suspect is never the one that did it. But just wait till I dig up some more ,clues. I'll turn up that clip, and Mr. Brundage, too."

"While you're waiting, you might just write down the list of things we have to do around here," said Jane sarcastically. "So we can divide 'em up and get done in time to go swimming afternoons. If we don't pitch in," she explained to Mike, "we're afraid our mother will just drag us all home, what with everything going to pieces and the tenants complaining their heads off all the time. You know, we might even try to fix some of the things they're complaining about, leaky faucets and stuff like that."

"How?" demanded Don. "You know perfectly well whenever anything goes wrong at home, we just complain to the landlord about it."

Jane burst out laughing, and after a moment, Don joined in. "It sure makes a difference," spluttered Jane, "whether you're the landlord or the tenant."

"I can do little repairs," said Mike cautiously.

"Mustn't monkey around with big jobs without a license, though. You can get in real trouble for that."

Jane and Don looked at him with respect. Imagine knowing what jobs you need a license for. But Jane said quickly: "Oh, we couldn't possibly ask you to help with stuff like that. What would you get out of it? It's not like happening along and helping with the lawn mower."

"And, boy, would we ever have been stuck if you hadn't," admitted Don.

"Well, I don't mind," said Mike slowly. "I'm used to being pretty busy, and I haven't got much of anything to do right now. Well, thanks for the lemonade." He stood up. "I might drop around some time and give you a hand with things."

"Gee, thank you for helping us all afternoon," said Jane.

"Be seeing you," said Don.

"Yeah," said Mike. He gave a hitch to his jeans, shook the hair back out of his eyes, and walked off toward the alley that led to the main street.

Jane looked out the door after him. "I hope he comes around often," she said. "Not just on account of helping, either. I think he's an awfully nice boy."

"Well, it's probably a novelty to him to see any-body under eighty years old," remarked Don. He pulled out his notebook and a pencil stub. "We might as well start making a list of the chores, if I can see to write in here."

"Ssh!" hissed Jane. "Here comes Betsy. We don't want her charging in here and upsetting paint and everything."

Betsy, carrying an old doll, wandered around the corner of the building. She looked sweet and rosy after her nap, and Mother had dressed her in a clean blue sunsuit. Victoria emerged from under the back steps, blinking at the sunlight; she stretched at great length, slowly, first the front legs and then the back, and rubbed around Betsy's ankles. It was just like a picture on a calendar, thought Jane: the little girl with the gold-colored curls, and the big cat with the silver-colored fur. Perfectly angelic. If you didn't happen to know better.

Don was thinking the same thing. "Somebody's got to do a job on keeping Betsy out of the tenants' hair," he whispered urgently. "Not just some of the time, *all* of the time. Because we're likely to have troubles enough of our own with the tenants, without Bets stirring 'em up any extra."

"She's already dumped sand on Mrs. Pennypacker's rug and eaten a box of Miss Giddings's raisins," admitted Jane. "And Victoria's been after the birds right under Miss Giddings's very nose. Well, I'll do the best I can, but don't think I'm going to spend all my time baby-sitting while you do the interesting jobs. You can just take turns on the baby-sitting, too!"

Odd Jobs Men

⚑ FIRST thing in the morning, Jane and Don studied the names and numbers on the mailboxes by the front door.

"If we're going to work around here, I guess we'll have to know which is who," said Jane. "We know some already. Pennypacker, number one. Giddings, number four. Five and six is us. Eight, Quincy. Dr.

Quincy, it says here, but Miss Giddings called him
Professor, so I guess he isn't the kind of doctor that
takes your tonsils out."

"He's a good guy," said Don. "What about all
these other names?"

"Mrs. Hand, number seven," read Jane. "That's
next down the hall from Great-great-uncle John's.
I've seen her coming out a couple of times. She
wears all black. Nine, Mr. and Mrs. Baker. Ten, Mr.
and Mrs. Blessing. I wouldn't have thought there
were that many men living here. Miss Amarilla
Smith, number two, next to Pennypacker. She's the
one that let Victoria out. Next to her, three, Mrs.
Broome. Oh, how funny!"

"What's funny about it?" demanded Don.

"Why, she's the one that was waving the broom
at poor Victoria! Imagine her being named Broome!
I'll be able to remember *that*, all right."

"They all look alike to me," said Don glumly.

The postman came in with his sack and dumped a
pile of letters and magazines on a little narrow table
under the mailboxes, and went out again, letting the
screen door slam. Miss Giddings's door opened a
crack; then she came out, closing the door behind
her, and tiptoed down the hall. She began shuffling
through the pile of mail.

"Now when Mr. Brundage was here," she began.

"What about Mr. Brundage?" asked Don alertly, reaching in his pocket for his notebook.

"He always sorted the mail and put it in the proper boxes. A very *obliging* young man, no matter what Myrtle Pennypacker—" She let the sentence trail off and carried her letters back to her apartment.

"Write it down," said Jane; and Don wrote, *Sort mail*. He already had two pages of daily chores and as many of the tenants' complaints as Mother could remember.

After sorting the mail, they went out back. There were noises coming out of the tool shed. They looked in, and there was Mike, picking through the contents of a flower pot, separating nails, fuses, and washers into three piles.

"Hi!" said Jane and Don.

"Hi!" he replied. "This place is a pig pen. Is it all right if I throw stuff in those big trash cans?"

"You bet," said Don. "What can we do?"

Mike promptly put them to work. He moved with decision through the mess, saving this and discarding that, until all the trash cans were full to overflowing and the shed began to take on some kind of order. He drove nails in the walls and hung up tools as he came across them; soon hammers, screwdrivers, pliers, wrenches, a saw, and a plane were hanging in a businesslike row. Cans of paint and putty that weren't dried out past using were neatly stacked in the old sink. Shutters, awnings, rolls of screen, coils of wire—he found a place for everything. The tool shed began to look twice as big, and a shaft of dusty sunlight came in through a little window that had been blocked by junk.

As they sorted through the mess, parts of an old croquet set kept turning up; and by the time they were finished, they had accumulated one end-post, five wobbly mallets, six balls, and quite a pile of wickets.

"Hot diggity!" remarked Don. "Just what we need." He set a croquet ball on the floor, took aim with a mallet, and swung. The head flew off the mallet, just missing Jane's ear, and the ball arched out through the door, crashed through a hibiscus bush, and thumped against the back of the apartment building. Victoria, every hair on end, shot out from under the bush and fled around the corner.

"Just what we don't need," said Jane coldly, picking up the mallet head and tossing it into a corner.

Don retrieved the ball. "No fooling, there's enough stuff here to have a good game of croquet," he argued.

"We could glue the mallets together and use the side lawn to set up the wickets. We wouldn't even have to move the chairs."

"Oh, sure, and have a couple of brittle tenants trip over the wickets and sue Mother for ten million dollars," Jane said scornfully. "Well, I guess this about does it." She tossed a handful of old dirty rags onto the top of a trash can.

Mike promptly rescued them. "You need rags for every kind of job, almost," he said reprovingly.

"Oh. Whatever for?"

"Clean off your hands. Mop up paint, or grease, or water. Now. I guess we're all set to start work."

"Start work?" repeated Don. "What have we just been doing?"

"Getting ready to work. What were some of these little jobs you were talking about?"

Jane protested: "Look here, Mike, you don't have to help us, you know. What I mean is, we have a special reason, or you bet we'd never be going out of our way to stir up any work."

"But I'd like to," Mike began. "Unless you don't want me to," he added, rather stiffly.

Before Jane could protest, Don said impatiently: "For Pete's sake, what are we standing around yakking about?" He pulled out his notebook. "Lemme see. Number seven. Who's that?"

"Mrs. Hand," said Jane.

"Well, it says here, the closet doorknob comes off."

"Lost the little screw that goes through the shank," guessed Mike. "What else?"

"Number one. Ugh, Mrs. Pennypacker. Pilot light on her stove doesn't work."

"Cleaning and adjusting."

"And number three, who's that?"

"Mrs. Broome," said Jane promptly.

"Well, one of her lamps goes on and off."

"What's wrong with that?" demanded Jane. "Lamps are supposed to go on and off."

"Listen, this lamp goes on when she turns it on, and then she's just sitting there minding her own business, and, zingo, it goes off again. Very mysterious."

"Loose connection somewhere inside," said Mike. "Anything else?"

"Yes, Quincy. Number eight. Kitchen door sticks. Won't close."

"Probably needs planing. If it's the top edge that sticks, it's simple. If it's the bottom, we take the door off the hinges. I guess that's enough for now."

"Let's do Pennypacker first and get it over with," suggested Don. "Maybe she isn't home," he added hopefully.

But she was. And before Don and Mike came out of her apartment, Mother called Jane to take charge of Betsy. Mother had to go to Mr. Merrill's office again; there were ever so many papers to sign before Great-great-uncle John's will could be probated, whatever that was. Apparently inheriting an apartment house was a complicated business; Jane only hoped that selling one would turn out to be just as complicated. ⟋

"If I'm not back in time for lunch, go ahead and fix yourselves something to eat," said Mother.

"Can I ask Mike to stay for lunch?" asked Jane.

"Mike?"

"You know, the boy that caught Victoria. He helped us with the lawn mower yesterday, and he's helping us again today. We like him."

"Of course you may ask him. Take care of Betsy, and don't let her—"

"Bother the tenants," finished Jane. "I won't."

There were three chair-sitters already under the big tree, and soon there would be more. Jane decided that the safest thing to do with Betsy was to take her right away from the place. So they went for a long exploring walk.

"Is this the way to the ocean?" Betsy kept asking, but Jane had something else in mind today. She took Betsy across the main street, over to the other side of town. They found streets of houses, little white and pink and sky-blue houses, each set in a tidy green lawn.

"I knew Palm Glade wasn't all old ladies," said Jane triumphantly.

"What?" asked Betsy.

"Nothing," said Jane.

Jane wandered along so slowly that Betsy had plenty of time to stoop and pick up chewing gum wrappers and other interesting objects and put them in her pockets. Jane was noting that there were play pens on the porches of the houses they passed, and swings and slides in the yards, and bicycles everywhere. Bicycles standing on the walks, and propped up against trees, and lying flat on lawns.

Half a dozen boys and girls, about Jane's own age, swooped past on bikes, laughing and talking. Jane looked sidewise at them, trying to guess which ones would be in her room at school. *If* she lived here, she added hastily to herself. If she lived here, she might

even have a bike of her own. At home, she had ridden
Ellen Schmidt's bike, a little; but the streets were
jammed with traffic and it was against the law to ride
on the sidewalks. But maybe, if she lived here—

"Oh, look!" she cried suddenly. "That must be
the school. Yes, it is. Come on."

On the school playground, there was a base-
ball game in progress, but Jane dragged Betsy right
through it, and they walked all around the building.
It wasn't a bit like the tall, dingy brick school at home.
This school was long and low, and painted pale green,
and one whole side was glass.

"Just the color of lime ice cream," said Jane. This
was a mistake, because Betsy promptly complained:
"I'm hungry."

"Just a little farther," coaxed Jane. "Then we'll go
back and get lunch."

Indeed, the town only went a little farther; they
came to railroad tracks and the street ended. Jane
looked across the tracks, but there were only sidings
and warehouses, and a few shacks and trailers. Beyond
that, Palm Glade just stopped.

On the way back, they passed a little stucco building with a big sign: Public Library. "Oh, Bets, a library, and we forgot to bring any books. I wonder if
I could get a card."

"Mike Mulligan," said Betsy hopefully. "Mrs. Tittlemouse. Johnny Crow's Garden." These were Betsy's favorite books, and she never got tired of listening to them, although Jane got very, very tired of reading them out loud to her.

Jane tried the door, but it was locked. Goodness, perhaps the library closed for the summer here, like the shops and hotels. She cupped her hands around her eyes and peered in through the glass panel. There were the rows of bookshelves, and the librarian's desk. Compared to the big city library where Mother worked, this was just a doll's house of a library. Instantly Jane decided that she liked this one better. She could see shelves of picture books, too tall to stand upright, lying on their sides; and a low table with little chairs, exactly the right size for Betsy.

"We can't get Mike Mulligan today," she told Betsy. "Maybe another time. Now we'll hurry home and have lunch."

Mother wasn't back yet, so Jane dumped a couple of cans of hash into a big skillet, added some leftover mashed potatoes to stretch it out, and let it heat while she sliced tomatoes and poured milk. Then she went to look for the boys.

The door to number eight was ajar, so she looked in. Mike and Don were busy sweeping up shavings, and Professor Quincy was gently swinging his kitchen door back and forth.

"Come in, come in," he called.

Jane took a firm hold on Betsy and stepped in. Why, it was more like a museum than a place to live in; everywhere she looked there were sea shells, sea shells in glass-topped cases, and on shelves and table tops, even on the window sills. They were of all sizes and shapes, and all colors, from plain brown and white to glowing rose and purple and iridescent blue.

"Oh, *beautiful!*" she breathed. "Where do they all come from?"

"Everywhere, just about," replied Professor Quincy. "Keep your eyes peeled at the beach and you can find a good many for yourself."

Jane pointed to a slender spiral, covered with fantastic sharp spines. "Could I find this?" she asked.

"Well, not likely," he admitted, his eyes twinkling. "Picked that up in the Solomon Islands. Had to dive for it, too. That's the Venus comb murex—*Murex tenuispina*. But any of these, now—" He pointed to a crowded table. "They're all our Gulf Stream natives, and as handsome as any."

Don and Mike finished sweeping and came and hung over the table with Jane. "This one's backward," said Mike suddenly, indicating a graceful twisted shell with pretty brown markings.

"You have sharp eyes," said Professor Quincy. "Yes, that fellow's *Busycon perversum*, the left-handed whelk. Curves in the opposite direction from any other shell. Nobody knows why."

"Say, we ought to start a collection," observed Don.

"See *my* collection!" Betsy piped up proudly. "Look!" She scrabbled around in her pocket and held out a handful of junk. Professor Quincy leaned solemnly over her palm and inspected it; among the scraps of shiny paper and glass were a few broken bits of shell.

He pointed to one of them, a gay orange, dappled with red. "A fine piece of pecten," he told her. "People call it the calico pecten, and its fancy name is *Pecten gibbus*. If you look carefully you can find perfect ones, shaped exactly like a little doll's fan."

"Thank you," said Jane, urging Betsy toward the door. "We have to go now."

But Betsy broke away and ran back. "And see *this!*" she added. "Does it have a fancy name, too?" She held out an old cigar butt, with the red-and-gold band still around it.

"Betsy!" cried Jane, covered with embarrassment. "Throw that nasty old thing away!"

But Professor Quincy just tugged at his little beard and examined the horrid object. "When this specimen was whole," he assured Betsy, "it must have been a very fine example of *Corona corona.*"

Back in number five, Jane invited Mike to stay for lunch. "It's only hash," she said, "but there's plenty of it. Maybe you'd better phone home and see if it's all right."

"Oh, it'll be all right," said Mike. "Thanks. Say, that Professor Quincy is swell, isn't he?"

"You bet," said Jane, moving the catsup out of Betsy's reach. "How did the other jobs go?"

"Fine!" exclaimed Don. "And, boy, am I ever learning things! The whole top of a stove comes right apart, did you know that?"

"Of course I know that," said Jane scornfully. "When something boils over, you have to take the stove apart to get it clean."

"Well, I never knew it before," admitted Don. "And then there's this little dingus you turn to make the pilot light higher or lower. Of course, Mrs. Pennypacker was breathing right down our necks the whole time. Guess it was to keep us from stealing whatever Mr. Brundage missed."

"Did she say anything more about her ruby clip?" asked Jane.

"Not to us," said Mike. "But some lady came to call for a few minutes, and she was telling her all about it. Said she's notified the insurance company."

"And I wrote it right down," added Don. "All that talk about how it was her poor dear mother's and she wouldn't take a million for it. Why, I wouldn't be surprised if she lost it on purpose so as to collect the insurance on it."

"Did you fix the lamp in number three?" asked Jane.

"Simple," said Don. "Nothing to it."

"And Mrs. Hand's doorknob?"

"That was simple, too. Screw loose. And if you ask me, that Mrs. Hand has a screw loose, too. You know what she said to us, when we walked in? She said: 'This is really a foreign country.'"

"*What!*" exclaimed Jane.

"She did, no fooling," Mike assured her.

"But—what did she mean?"

"Boy, we didn't ask," said Don. "We just fixed that doorknob and got out of there. It was really spooky, all the shades down. I told you there were some pretty sinister characters right in this building," he added darkly.

"Well, anyway, Professor Quincy isn't sinister,"

Professor Quincy examined the horrid object.

said Jane. "He's nice. And I bet he's been all over all the oceans in the whole world."

"Hey, speaking of oceans, how about us going s-w-i-m-m-i-n-g?" Don spelled the word out. "Is you-know-who having a n-a-p or do we have to drag her along?"

Betsy looked suspiciously from Don to Jane. "What are you spelling about?" she demanded. "Tell me!"

"Nothing," said Jane soothingly. "Come on, we'll lie down on the bed and I'll tell you a story until Mother gets home."

"I'll listen," said Betsy coldly. "But I won't lie down and I won't shut my eyes and I won't take a nap."

"Come on across to number six," said Don to Mike. "I think I've got some old s-w-i-m-m-i-n-g t-r-u-n-k-s that'll fit you."

By the time Mother returned, Betsy was asleep, and Jane and Don and Mike were waiting impatiently, all ready to go swimming. Jane introduced Mike to Mother; and she was relieved to see how politely he stood up and shook hands. Then she was ashamed of herself for being relieved. After all, just because a person needed a haircut didn't mean he didn't have any manners.

Mother was doubtful about letting them go swimming where there weren't any lifeguards, or even any grownups. "But, Mother," protested Jane. "Don and I have been swimming for years."

"But only in pools," Mother pointed out. "The ocean must be much more dangerous."

"But it was just as calm yesterday, and shallow as anything at the edge. And besides, Mike's used to the ocean; aren't you, Mike?"

Mother looked at Mike. Mike looked embarrassed. Then he brightened up. "I passed my Junior Lifesaving last year," he said. "Honest I did. Of course, I haven't exactly saved any lives. Yet." .

Mother laughed. "I hope you don't have a chance to. Well, all right. Don't swim out beyond your depth."

"We won't!" they chorused.

"And keep together."

"We will!"

"And if it's rough, don't go in at all."

"We won't!"

Then they shot out the door before Mother could change her mind.

A Ramp for Mr. Blessing

🐾 THE next week was a busy one. Mike showed up nearly every day, and after they were through with their jobs they went swimming. A couple of times they had to take Betsy with them, because Mother had appointments with Mr. Merrill or with real estate agents who were anxious to sell 303 Oleander Drive. And for a whole week Betsy was as good as gold, playing happily by herself, hour after hour.

"What is this 'biscuit bush' she keeps talking about?" asked Mother.

"She's fixed a little play place under one of the hibiscus bushes," Jane explained. "She has it all decorated up with busted shells and bottle caps and all those awful things she's always picking up. She plays house in there with her doll. And with Victoria, too, whenever she can catch her."

But one day when Jane went to look for Betsy, the biscuit bush was empty. Betsy was perched on a chair under the big tree, right in the middle of a group of chair-sitters, chattering her head off. Her hair was in a dreadful snarl, full of twigs and leaves, and her face and hands and knees were filthy.

"Betsy! Come here!" called Jane.

Betsy ignored her. So Jane had to walk over and pick Betsy up and carry her off. "I'm sorry she's been bothering you," she called back over her shoulder to the chair-sitters.

"But we were having a lovely time," Betsy protested. "We were visiting."

"Those ladies don't like children to visit them," said Jane firmly. "Those ladies don't like children, period. We'll find something else to do. Let's go around on the other side and water the bushes with the hose."

"All right," said Betsy. "They did too like me to visit them," she added sulkily.

"I bet," muttered Jane under her breath, as she went around back and turned on the water. But when she returned to where Betsy was holding the nozzle, no water was coming out of it.

"There must be a kink in it somewhere," said Jane. "Wait here. I'll go fix it." She traced the hose back to the faucet, but there were no kinks anywhere. She tried the faucet handle again. Yes, it was turned on, all the way. "Still no water?" she shouted to Betsy.

"No water!" Betsy shouted back.

Oh, dear, something else for the boys to fix; Jane only hoped that Mike would know what to do about it, because Don certainly wouldn't. She went in the building to look for the boys, and met them coming out of number ten, carrying wrenches and looking very pleased with themselves.

"No water's coming out of the hose," she reported.

"Sure, we know," said Don. "We just fixed a leaky faucet for the Blessings, and we had to turn the water off."

"But not the *hose* water, too!"

"Sure," said Mike. "We had to take the faucet off, and the water cut-off in the apartment didn't work, so we turned off the water for the whole building. There's a place outside, where the main comes in from the street."

"And listen!" Don cried excitedly. "Wait till you hear the swell idea Mike just had."

"Tell me later," said Jane crossly. "You turn on that water before everybody comes swarming out to complain."

"O.K. Keep your shirt on," said Don amiably. "Water coming right up."

Jane started back to Betsy. Betsy had dragged the hose up to the front corner of the building and was waving it happily around, like a jump rope, chanting:

> "Last *night*,
> The night before,
> A lemon and a *pickle*—"

Just as she said *pickle*, two things happened, both at once. Mrs. Pennypacker walked out the front door of the building. And the water suddenly shot out of the hose nozzle, full force.

It might have been much worse, the way Betsy was waving the hose around. Mrs. Pennypacker was really lucky that the water didn't hit her right in the face, instead of just getting her shoes and stockings and the hem of her dress wet. She didn't act lucky, though. She acted very unpleasant, although Jane said over and over again that it was an accident and that she was sorry.

When Mrs. Pennypacker finally closed her mouth in a tight angry line, and turned to go back in and change her clothes, Betsy called after her reassuringly: "It's only water! Look, *I'm* not scared to get wet!"

And Betsy turned the hose squarely on her own middle, soaking herself from top to bottom. This was the last straw. After Jane had mopped and changed Betsy and turned her over to Mother, she went out to find the boys and tell them what she thought about people who turn water off and on without warning.

Don and Mike were sorting through a pile of old boards behind the tool shed. "Look, this is Mike's idea!" shouted Don. "We're building a ramp."

"A what?"

"You know, a ramp. A slanting runway, for a wheel chair."

"Whatever for?"

"For Mr. Blessing. We were just in there, and he's a very nice guy, only he has to stay in a wheel chair, so he can't ever get outside. Mr. Brundage used to carry him down the front steps, wheel chair and all, but Mrs. Blessing isn't strong enough to do that. And neither are we. So Mike said, look, we'll build you a ramp to go over the steps, and anybody can just push the wheel chair up and down it. Isn't that a swell idea?"

It was, but Jane didn't feel like admitting it. "It'll look perfectly awful," she said. "And what will the other tenants say about it?"

"We won't have to leave it there all the time," explained Mike. "We're going to fix it so it can be set in place, and then carried away and stored out here when he isn't using it. Besides, it won't look so awful if we do a neat job on it. We might even paint it to match the steps."

"But you're not going to do all that *now*, are you?" exclaimed Jane. "I thought we were going swimming."

"I know, but we sort of promised we'd get on this job right away," said Don. "It's going to be fun. Look, you can stick around and help us, if you want."

"Oh sure, I can run and fetch your tools, and hold the boards together while you nail them," said Jane coldly. "No thanks. I'm sure you'll get along just fine without me."

She stormed into the building, blinking back angry tears. Boys always get the best of everything, all the big interesting jobs, things you can stand back and look at when you're finished. And what was left for her? Same old dishes, dirty again the minute you get them washed. Same old beds, rumpled again the minute you get them smooth. And keep an eye on Betsy and get blamed for everything she does.

Jane ran down the dim corridor and almost knocked Mrs. Hand down, as she stood outside the door of number seven, fumbling with her key.

"Oh, I'm terribly sorry," said Jane hastily. "I didn't even see you."

"I don't show up very well, do I?" murmured Mrs. Hand, glancing down at her black dress. She looked at Jane's stormy face, and added: "I wonder if you would do me a favor, my dear, and unlock my door. It is really very difficult for me to see the keyhole."

"We're going to put in stronger light bulbs, but we haven't got around to it yet," said Jane. She took the key and unlocked the door, and the funny thing was, she felt a little better already, in a confused way.

"Thank you," said Mrs. Hand. "Perhaps you will do me another favor? I am just going to make myself a cup of tea, and it would give me great pleasure if you would join me."

"Oh, I would just love to," said Jane, and the minute she said it, she knew it was true. Mrs. Hand led the way into the darkened apartment; instead of raising a blind, she snapped on a lamp that spread a soft yellow glow over the room.

"It's cozier this way," she explained.

Jane stared all around at the silk hangings and painted scrolls that covered the walls, at the shelves of glowing bowls and vases, at the little carved statues on the low tables. "Oh," she gasped. "It's—it's like another country."

"It is another country," smiled Mrs. Hand. "It's a very small piece of China, where I was born and lived most of my life."

"Oh. But you're not Chinese. Or are you?" added Jane doubtfully. Mrs. Hand's hair was snow white, and her small, delicate, wrinkled face might be almost anything; but surely, with those bright blue eyes—

"Oh, no. I am American, although I spoke Chinese before I spoke English. But I said we should have tea, and so we shall." Jane followed her into the kitchen, which she was surprised to see was exactly like the kitchen in number five. "No, this is not Chinese," said Mrs. Hand, lighting the gas under the teakettle. "It is pure Palm Glade, thank goodness. I have cooked over a charcoal fire in a brick stove, but I can't say I really enjoyed it, even when I was younger."

Jane sat and drank hot unsweetened tea out of a thin cup without a handle, and Mrs. Hand told her what the painted Chinese characters on the cup meant. At first Jane just looked and looked at all the strange and beautiful things around her; then she began to ask questions, shyly at first. Mrs. Hand sipped her tea and answered the questions in her soft voice, and one thing led to another. Soon Jane was listening, entranced, to stories about Mrs. Hand's childhood among the bare brown hills of North China, where the camel caravans set out at dusk to cross the great Gobi Desert. And stories about the mission hospital where Mrs. Hand's husband had doctored the Chinese from miles and miles around.

Jane held the little bowl-like cup between her hands until the tea was quite cold, and listened with shining eyes. When she finally realized how long she had stayed and stood up to go, she was so stiff that she knew she must have sat all that time without moving, just listening.

"Thank you for the tea," she said. "And for the stories. I'd love to come again, some time, if I may."

"Please do," said Mrs. Hand, smiling. "And bring your brothers, if they aren't too busy. They were so kind to mend that miserable doorknob for me, but they left in such a hurry that I didn't even have a chance to thank them." Before Jane could explain that only one of the boys was her brother, Mrs. Hand added: "And your sweet little sister. It cheers me up,

Jane listened with shining eyes.

just to watch her trotting about so busily with her sunny hair. I hadn't realized, until you came, how sadly we have missed having any children around here."

"Thank you, they'd love to come, I know," said Jane. "And thank you again for everything."

Jane ran out back, where Don and Mike were working away on the ramp. "How's it coming?" she asked.

"It's a bigger job than I thought," said Mike. "We had to work on it around front for a while, to get the angle right. See, these blocks will fit onto the steps and keep it from slipping."

"It's going to look very nice," said Jane generously. "And it was really swell of you to think of doing it." She waited a minute to give them a chance to ask her where she had been, but they just went right on working. "I've been in visiting Mrs. Hand," she remarked casually.

"The crazy one? Were we right about her, or were we right?" mumbled Don through a mouthful of nails.

"I don't see how you could have been wronger if you'd tried for a year," replied Jane. "She's the most wonderful person I ever met, and she's had the most exciting adventures you ever heard. She's a retired missionary and—"

"Retired missionary?" hooted Don. "*Exciting?*"

"Of course, it might not be exciting enough for you," said Jane loftily. "But when she was a little girl, she was kidnapped by bandits and hidden in an old abandoned temple and held for ransom. And she has walked along the top of the Great Wall of China, and she has crossed the Gobi Desert on a camel, with a caravan; and a few years ago she stopped a whole army of soldiers, single-handed, from looting a hospital."

"Single-handed? *Her?*" exclaimed Don.

"How?" asked Mike. "With a machine gun?"

"With an apple pie," replied Jane.

"An apple pie? What did she do, throw it?" demanded Don.

"No, she just baked it, and that stopped them," replied Jane coolly. "But of course it's not exciting enough for you."

Don tossed his hammer aside and sat down. "Well, go on. We're asking. Besides, you're just dying to tell."

"We need a rest anyway," said Mike.

"All right. Well, it wasn't so many years ago, just before she retired and came back to this country, and she was living at this mission hospital where her husband used to be the head doctor before he died. There was fighting and looting and trouble all over China, and the people at the hospital knew that they would have to pull out sooner or later, but they hated to leave their patients, so they hung on and hung on. Then one day, a Chinese farmer came running to tell them that there were soldiers in the neighborhood. So the Americans and the Chinese doctors and nurses began bundling things together—anything they could carry that would help them go on with their work somewhere else. But just then a whole mob of soldiers came stamping into the courtyard. Did I say it was a very confused time? Anyway, it was hard to tell who was fighting who, and some of the soldiers weren't exactly fighting anybody—just rampaging around killing people and stealing anything they could lay hands on. And of course they could always sell stuff like penicillin and surgical instruments.

"Well. So here came all these soldiers, and the leader banged on the door with his gun. Well, Mrs. Hand told the other hospital people to go ahead with what they were doing, and she went to the door and opened it. You know how tiny she is? Well, so she just stood there, right in the middle of the doorway, so the officer couldn't get in without shoving her. And it seems that in China old people are very much respected, and he couldn't shove Mrs. Hand without losing face, or something. So he bowed, and addressed her as Venerable Old Woman, which is the proper thing to say, and asked after her health. And she bowed, and asked after *his* health. And he asked her if she was English. And she said, no, she was American. And he said that once he had paid a visit to America.

"So then she said politely that she hoped he had brought away pleasant memories of America, and he said the pleasantest memory he had brought away was about apple pie. And he said he had never tasted any apple pie since. So she bowed again, and said that she would be honored to bake him a genuine apple pie, if he would condescend to sample her unworthy cooking. And he answered that he was too unworthy to put such a Venerable Old Woman to all that trouble. Mrs. Hand says that you absolutely have to talk this way in China if you are well brought up, and she says the officer must have been well brought up in spite of being a sort of bandit leader.

"So in the end, he told his soldiers to wait there in the courtyard, and she invited him in and sat him down, and then she fired up the stove and baked him an apple pie. And you know how long *that* takes! And by the time he had eaten that whole pie, every bite of it, the other hospital people had bundled up everything valuable and escaped out the back way with it and headed for the mountains, and the soldiers never did catch up with them!"

"Hot diggity!" exclaimed Don in admiration. He looked at Mike, and they both grinned sheepishly.

"I guess maybe we were wrong about Mrs. Hand," admitted Mike.

"I guess maybe you were," said Jane smugly. "But cheer up, I'll never tell her what you said about her, and if you're very good, I might even take you to visit her some day."

"Another good clue gone," said Don mournfully, pulling out his notebook. "I sure had her way up on my list of suspects. Thought she was peculiar enough to do anything." He flipped through the pages. "Look, now we've done something for every single tenant in the building except Miss Giddings, and she's never complained about anything. I wonder why."

Mike snapped his fingers. "I meant to tell you, but I forgot. Thought it might be a clue. The lady next door to Mrs. Pennypacker—what's her name?"

"Smith," said Jane.

"Yeah, Miss Smith. She grabbed me the other day and asked me to come in and take a look at her refrigerator because it wasn't freezing ice or anything.

She was playing canasta with Mrs. Pennypacker, and both of them were talking about dear Lucy. Took me a while to figure it out, but dear Lucy is Miss Giddings."

"What were they saying about her?" asked Don, licking his pencil.

"Well, all about how dear Lucy was always glad enough to come to *their* apartments and play canasta and eat their refreshments, but she never invited them into *her* apartment."

"Not ever?" asked Jane.

"Well, I wouldn't know about not ever," said Mike cautiously, "but not since either of them could remember."

"That's peculiar, all right," said Don, writing it down. "But if all this has been going on for years and years, I don't see how we can connect it up with something that only happened last week, like stealing that ruby clip."

"Or suspect her of hiding Mr. Brundage in her apartment," giggled Jane.

"More likely she just never makes the bed or does the dishes, and she doesn't want anybody to find out about it," suggested Don.

"Oh, Don—*Miss Giddings!*" exclaimed Jane. "Why, anybody can tell, just to look at her, that she's the type to make the bed with hospital corners and rinse the dishes with boiling water and dust the places that don't even show!"

"Look, all I did was write it down. I haven't deduced anything about it yet. I've been writing everything down. Look at all the stuff I've got about Mr. Brundage, and none of it any good. I sure wish we could find him, he's the key to this whole thing."

"What do you mean, none of it's any good?" asked Mike.

"Well, it's all different. Listen. Miss Giddings thought he was the nicest young man, so helpful and obliging. Professor Quincy didn't think he was so young, but then he hardly noticed him at all. Miss Smith thought he was a northerner, as he didn't have a southern accent, but then hardly anybody around here does. They all come from somewhere else. Mr. and Mrs. Blessing thought he was just wonderful to them, and to Great-great-uncle John, too. I guess Great-great-uncle John was pretty sick, but he was stubborn about having a doctor or going to the hospital, and Mr. Brundage took care of him."

"He sounds nice," said Jane. "That must be the reason things were in such a mess around here. Poor Mr. Brundage was too busy playing nurse to do anything else."

"And Mrs. Pennypacker," Don went on, "thought he was rude and impertinent and she wouldn't be surprised if he turned out to be an escaped convict."

"She thinks that about everybody," said Jane.

"And every single solitary one of them has a different idea about what color eyes and hair he has and what he looks like in general," Don finished up, closing the notebook. "So you can see why it's no good. Now if this was only happening in a book, there would be a busted clock stopped at 11:32, and somebody would have seen a man with red hair, a wooden leg, and mermaids tattooed on both arms."

"By the way," said Jane to Mike, "what did turn out to be the matter with Miss Smith's refrigerator?"

"She was right about it. It wasn't freezing or any thing," said Mike solemnly. "She'd knocked the plug out of the socket, sweeping behind it. I just plugged it back in again."

Who Stole the Beans?

THE very next day, they turned up another clue for Don to write down.

Mother was having lunch at a restaurant with a real estate man. Business in Palm Glade was dull in the summer, and all the real estate agents in town were falling over themselves trying to make some kind of a deal on 303 Oleander Drive. First they had to persuade some client that he wanted to buy it, and then they had to persuade Mother that she wanted to sell it. "What can they lose?" demanded Don. "Whatever happens, they get their commission."

He and Mike and Jane went in to see about lunch. Mike always stayed for lunch now, and Jane couldn't help wondering how he stayed so thin, he ate so much.

"Somebody better get to the grocery store pretty soon," she said. "But at least, there's that can of beans, and plenty of oranges and bread and butter and milk. Say, where *is* that can of beans?"

"We probably ate it," said Don.

"We couldn't have. It was right here yesterday, because I caught Betsy peeling the label off it, and I took it away from her and put it on the top shelf, and now it's gone."

Everybody looked at Betsy.

"I did not either take it," said Betsy. "Jane put it up too high and I couldn't reach."

"Ha!" said Don, and he whipped out his notebook and wrote down: Missing, one can of beans. "Not that I can see what help that is," he admitted.

"Well, somebody took it," said Jane crossly. "So now we'll just have to fill up on bread and butter.

I suppose anybody could just walk in, because we hardly ever bother to lock the door."

"No peanut butter?" asked Don.

"No."

"No jelly?"

"No."

"Just naked bread and butter?"

"I don't want my bread and butter naked," complained Betsy. "Put catsup on it."

"Hey, that's not a bad idea, and here's a whole bottle of catsup!" cried Don. So they had catsup sandwiches for lunch, and they were surprisingly good, with plenty of cold milk.

The next morning, Jane and Don collected the trash baskets, as usual, from outside the apartment doors. Jane was emptying one into the big outdoor trash can, when suddenly she let out a yell: "The missing can!" She snatched it out of the trash. "Look, half the label is torn off, slantwise. That's exactly the way Betsy tore it before I took it away from her. And here it is, in Miss Giddings's trash."

As soon as Mike came around, they took him into the tool shed and showed him the can and told him about it. "But I don't really see what sense it makes," said Jane, "because I simply can't imagine Miss Giddings sneaking around stealing canned beans. Can you?"

"Maybe she's a kelp—klep—what's that word that means you steal things because you can't help it? It's a sort of a disease," explained Mike.

"Kleptomaniac!" shouted Don. "Say, that's it! This begins to add up now. The reason Miss Giddings never lets anyone into her apartment is because it's loaded with all the stuff she's been stealing for years!"

"There's something wrong with that," objected Jane. "I read somewhere about kleptomaniacs, and they never use the things they steal. They just take 'em to be taking 'em."

"Well, you haven't noticed Miss Giddings wearing that ruby clip around, have you?" asked Don triumphantly.

"No, but whoever took those beans ate 'em. The can was scraped clean. A kleptomaniac would more likely just keep the whole thing, beans and all. Besides, I just can't see Miss Giddings wolfing down a whole can of beans. She's more the tea and toast type."

"Oh, you and your types. Miss Giddings is the hottest suspect we've got yet."

"Well, I'll admit that she's a little peculiar, but I'm beginning to like her, almost. *Oh!*" exclaimed Jane suddenly. "I'm sitting on the *awnings!*"

"Sure you are. You always sit on 'em and leave me and Mike the uncomfortable places to sit."

"But, look, I hung these out on the line last night, to air. They're so musty they smell awful. Did you bring them in here this morning?"

"Me? What for?" asked Don, in bewilderment.

"Well, I didn't, and Mike didn't because we grabbed him the minute he came, and Betsy didn't because she couldn't even reach the clothesline, and Mother didn't because she hasn't been outside today. And you know Miss Giddings wouldn't touch the smelly old things with a ten-foot pole," continued Jane excitedly. "But *somebody* did. Say, what if Mr. Brundage has come back, and is keeping under cover and sleeping in our tool shed! These would make a fine bed, if you could stand the smell."

"That's it! That's it!" shouted Don. "And he sneaked into number five and swiped our beans and ate 'em!"

"They were his own beans," Jane pointed out. "They've been in the cupboard ever since we came. And how could you say he sneaked in when that's his own apartment?"

"All right, all right, but then why doesn't he walk right in and say, look, everybody, I'm back?" demanded Don, writing furiously in his notebook.

"Maybe he came back, and somehow overheard something about that ruby clip, and how Mrs. Pennypacker thinks he stole it," said Jane slowly. "And then, maybe he thought it would be a good idea to find out what the score is before he shows himself. And maybe he's even trying to find the clip himself, to prove he didn't steal it. Or something like that."

"Whatever he's up to, this is a red-hot clue, and the sooner we follow it up the better. I'm going to keep an eye on the tool shed and catch whoever moved those awnings if it takes all night."

"I'll watch with you," said Jane. "You can keep an eye on the tool shed, and I'll keep an eye on you. Good thing Mother is sleeping across the hall with Betsy, because if there would be anything worse than Mother finding out about this, it would be Betsy waking up and trailing after us."

Mike insisted on coming back after dark to help, although they said they could handle it by themselves. "If you're going to nab Mr. Brundage tonight, I want to be in on it," he said firmly.

At bedtime, Jane and Don went over to number six, as usual, and turned out the light. Then they watched the crack under Mother's door until the light went out, and they gave her a little extra time to get to sleep. Then they slipped out the back door.

Mike was there ahead of them, standing in the shadow of the big palm outside Jane's window. "Nothing doing yet," he whispered.

The three of them separated and hid in different places, so that they could see not only the tool shed but most of the grounds as well. There was a full moon, skittering in and out of clouds. They could see fairly well in the open spaces, but the shadows were inky black. For some time there was nothing stirring, except several hundred mosquitoes, all of them apparently starving to death.

JANE saw the man first. He was standing in the shadow of the big live oak. While Jane watched, he walked over to a coconut palm and stood in its shadow. Jane couldn't see much of anything except his shape, but he walked like a young man. Much younger, anyway, than any of the tenants of 303 Oleander Drive.

Taking advantage of all the shadows, she crept back to the corner of the building; then she ran to tell Don and Mike. They all three ran back to the corner and peered around it. The man had moved to another

Jane saw the man first.

tree; he went on walking, from tree to tree, until he reached the far edge of the lawn. Then he set off up the street at a brisk pace.

"He's not coming; he's going," whispered Don, in a disappointed voice.

Jane wasn't disappointed. She had had plenty of time for thinking, standing around in the dark and slapping at mosquitoes; and she was beginning to wonder what they would do about Mr. Brundage if they did catch him. No matter how nice the Blessings said he was, after all they really didn't know a thing about him. "Let's go back to bed," she whispered.

"No, let's follow him and see where he goes," urged Mike.

They followed silently, keeping about a block behind and on the opposite side of the street, but the man never looked back. He walked rapidly for several blocks, right over to the neighborhood of little houses that Jane had explored; and he turned in at one of them. He walked straight up to the door, put a key in the lock, and went in. A moment later, lights showed at several windows.

Don and Mike crept up to the windows, but the blinds were drawn to the sills and they couldn't see a thing. Don wrote down the address and they all started back.

"None of this makes any sense," grumbled Don. "Why would he be sleeping in our tool shed if he has a place like that to stay?"

"*If* that's Mr. Brundage," said Mike.

"And he has a key and he turned on a light, so it doesn't look as if he had broken in while the owners were away," said Jane.

"I don't care who he is, there's something awfully fishy about him," insisted Don. "Why would any honest man be sneaking around our yard at night? And keeping in the tree shadows all the time, too."

Jane yawned so hard her jaws cracked. "Let's worry about it tomorrow," she mumbled.

They said good night to Mike on the main street. "I hope you don't catch it from your folks, coming in at this hour," said Don.

"Oh, I'll be all right," answered Mike. "See you tomorrow."

Next morning, before they even did their chores, Don insisted on going back to the little bungalow. "But what for?" asked Jane. "You can't just knock on the door and ask that man what he was doing under our trees last night."

"Well, I can hang around and get a good look at him by daylight, and find out where he goes when he comes out," said Don stubbornly.

"Then wait till Mike comes around. You'll do something silly if you go by yourself."

"I can't wait, he'll be out of the house and gone by then," argued Don.

"Then I'll come with you. But what are you going to do—just stand around out front and goggle at the house?"

"We'll think of something. Come on." When they reached the house, Don pulled a handful of marbles from his pocket and drew a circle at the sandy edge of the street. "You can shoot first," he offered.

"Marbles. Ugh, I hate marbles," said Jane. "It hurts my knees and besides you always win."

Don won all the marbles, and gave back half of them, and won them all again, before the house door opened and a man came out, carrying a brief case. He set off down the street.

"Do you suppose that's him?" whispered Jane, as they hastily gathered up the marbles.

"He's about the same size, and he walks the same way," replied Don. "We'll see where he goes, anyway."

They followed along behind. At the first corner the man stopped at a mail box and dropped a letter in; then he walked briskly on.

"Hey, look!" exclaimed Jane. "He's turning in at

our place. Why, he walked right in the front door!"

They broke into a run, but although they dashed into the building almost at his heels, the hall was empty. "He didn't have time to go through and out the back," whispered Don excitedly. "He must be in one of the apartments."

"That's right," agreed Jane. "But whose?"

All the apartment doors were closed, and beside each door was a trash basket. "We haven't collected the trash yet," said Don in a low voice. "We'll do it now, and listen at each door. Whoever that guy is, and whatever he's up to, somebody in this building is in cahoots with him."

They took turns emptying the trash, so that one of them remained inside watching the closed doors. In five minutes they were finished, and they hadn't heard a sound inside any of the doors except the clink of breakfast dishes being washed.

"I'll get out under the bushes and do a little sleuthing through the windows," whispered Don. "You stay here and watch."

Jane stood around in the hall, feeling silly. Professor Quincy took in his trash basket and set off on his regular morning walk. Miss Giddings opened her door, just wide enough to take in the trash basket, and closed it again; Jane heard the lock click. Mrs.

Pennypacker turned on her radio, and somebody further up the hall started a vacuum cleaner.

Then a door at the far end of the hall opened, and the man they had been following walked out, and walked down the hall past Jane, and on out the front door.

Jane just stared after him without moving. Don dashed into the building. "Say, look alive!" he hissed. "He just came out! Which apartment?"

Jane pointed. "Ours," she said.

"What! You must be crazy. I'll ask Mother." They went into number five. Mother was just starting to clear away the breakfast dishes, and Betsy was trailing a hair ribbon across the floor for Victoria to chase.

"Mother! Was there a man in here just now?" demanded Don breathlessly.

"Why, yes," replied Mother. "Jane, you're just in time. Would you rather wash or wipe?"

"But, Mother, who was he?" cried Don.

"Goodness, don't shout so. He's Mr. Remington, that real estate agent who took me to lunch the other day. He has a client up north that seems interested in the property, a man with a lot of money who might remodel the place and turn it into a luxury apartment for winter rentals. The man keeps writing and asking him questions, and the latest was, would there be room to put a swimming pool on the grounds without sacrificing too many trees. Mr. Remington wanted to get an air mail answer in the morning collection, so he says he came around last night and paced it off, and he thinks there is."

Jane and Don just looked at each other, feeling very, very foolish. "Oh," said Don lamely. "I just wondered."

"I hope you aren't going to sell it to him," said Jane anxiously.

"Well, not right this very minute," replied Mother. "As a matter of fact, I've had several offers, but Mr. Merrill tells me they are all far below the actual value of the place. The buyers all hope I'll sell it for a song, just to get it off my hands. And I might have, too, if you hadn't been such a big help. How would you like to take the day off? I'll pack a lunch, and you can spend the whole day at the beach."

"Oh, Mother, that would be wonderful!" cried Jane, giving Mother a big hug. "Pack enough for Mike, too. And we'll take Betsy with us, and that will give you the day off, too!" she offered, in a sudden burst of generosity.

Tenants Are People

◤ JANE and Don both helped with the dishes, and then they hurried through their chores while Mother packed the lunch. They sorted the mail, and Jane vacuumed the hall carpet, and Don swept the walks and picked up a couple of dead coconut fronds from the lawn. And still Mike hadn't shown up.

"I wish he'd hurry," complained Jane. "If we only

knew where he lives, we could go by and pick him up."

"You know what I bet?" asked Don. "I bet he got caught coming in last night, late, and he's being punished today and they won't let him out."

"You're probably right," said Jane gloomily. "I think his parents must be perfectly awful. Look how he needs a haircut, and those awful old jeans haven't been washed since we met him. And I don't think he has any bathing things. He always wears those old trunks of yours."

"Maybe they're only poor," said Don. "That's no crime."

"I don't think Mike would care about that, if only they were halfway nice. But look how he spends so much time here, and yet he's never invited us to his house. Not even once."

Don burst out laughing. "You sound exactly like Mrs. Pennypacker, giving poor dear Lucy a good going over!" he snorted.

"I do not!" cried Jane furiously. "It's different, because I like Mike, and Mrs. Pennypacker doesn't like anybody. But if he lives where I think he lives, I guess he doesn't want to invite us to come there or meet his parents," she added, thinking of the slovenly shacks and battered trailers on the other side of the tracks.

"Maybe you're right, and they're perfect stinkers. The only thing is—look how much he knows and how many things he can do. I bet anybody that had been really kicked around wouldn't be able to do all the things Mike can, and do them so well."

The more Jane thought about this, the more sense it made. She looked at Don almost respectfully. "Well, I wish we could do something for him, after all the things he's done for us. I guess all we can do is feed him plenty and try to be extra nice to him."

"For Pete's sake, don't be too nice to him, or we'll never see him again!" exclaimed Don in alarm. "If you start sloshing all over him, he'll suspect that we're sorry for him, and nobody can stand people being sorry for them."

"Ssh, here he comes now," warned Jane.

They greeted him with the latest news about the mysterious night prowler, and Mike grinned. "I don't think it's so funny," growled Don. "All that work for nothing, and what's the guy doing? Pacing off a swimming pool. For two bits I'd go out of the detecting business right now."

"You can go out of it for today, because we're

going to the ocean," Jane reminded him. "And we can stay as long as we want. Unless Betsy gets fussy without any nap."

They got their bathing suits off the line, and Don and Mike changed in number six, while Jane helped Mother get Betsy ready.

"Take good care of Betsy," said Mother, handing Jane the lunch.

"Well, she may get sunburned, but she certainly won't get drowned," Jane assured her. "She hardly even gets her feet wet. All she wants to do is dig in the sand."

It was a perfect day, with a hot sun and a cool breeze, and big white pudding clouds stacked up at the far edge of the ocean. Betsy made sand cities, and Jane and Don and Mike splashed and swam and came out and lay on the hot sand, and swam some more.

"Boy, this sure beats that old crowded pool back home!" exclaimed Don.

"With somebody else's feet always in your face and your eyes full of chlorine," agreed Jane.

Nobody had a watch, so they ate lunch when they got hungry. The breeze from the ocean blew a little fine sand into everything, but nobody really minded.

"There's a trick to it," announced Don, chomping solemnly. "When you chew, don't bring your teeth together all the way. That way you can chew things up enough to swallow 'em, and still not go scrunch, scrunch on the sand."

Mother had put up a perfectly enormous lunch, and Jane didn't see how they could possibly finish it all, but Mike polished off the last two sandwiches and the left-over devilled eggs with no effort at all. They don't even feed him enough at home, Jane thought indignantly; but out loud she only said: "We'll have to wait at least an hour before we go in the water again."

So they turned to and built Betsy a big, fancy sand castle just above the water's edge. It had towers of all shapes and sizes, and an outer wall and an inner wall and a moat and a drawbridge, and Mike scouted up and down the beach and collected dozens of shells to trim it with.

He examined each shell carefully before he stuck it on the castle. "These sunset shells are the prettiest," he said enthusiastically. "Look, the stripes on some are pinkish, and others are more purplish. All the shiny ones this shape are tellins. This one's *Tellina radiata*." He stumbled over the name, and then blushed as Don and Jane gaped at him.

"Gee, how did you learn that?" asked Don, impressed.

"Well, I've been in to look at Professor Quincy's shells quite a few times, and I try to remember what he tells me. But, gee, there's thousands of 'em, and they all have these fancy long names. The best way would be to have a book to look 'em up in."

"Professor Quincy has stacks of big books about shells, with pictures, too," said Don. "I bet he'd let you borrow one, if you asked."

"Maybe, but I wouldn't have any place to keep a book," began Mike, and then stopped uncomfortably, as if he had said something he didn't mean to. He ducked his head down and got very busy, sticking shells on the castle wall in a fancy design.

I bet he doesn't have any place to keep a book, thought Jane. I bet he never has had a book of his own. "You could use the library a lot," she suggested helpfully. "You ought to see the piles of reference books in the library where Mother works. Of course, they don't let you take them out, but you can look at them all you want. Oh, I forgot, the library here is closed for the summer."

"I bet Professor Quincy likes you to look at his books," said Don. "And ask questions, too. He used to be a college professor, Mother says, and he's one of the world's greatest authorities on shells and the animals that live in 'em. You'd never think it to look at him, would you?"

"Gee, that's what I'd like to do, if I could," said Mike eagerly. "Collect shells and find out all about 'em."

"Sure you could," said Don. "You just go to college and learn all you can out of other people's books, and when you get really good, you write books for other people to study." Mike's face clouded over, and Don added hastily: "You don't have to have lots of money to go to college. Lots of people work their way through."

Mike went off to gather more shells, without answering, and Jane whispered fiercely to Don: "Quit talking about going to college. Fat chance Mike has, with those awful parents of his. They'll probably make him quit school and get a job, and grab every cent he makes."

Betsy tried to help with the sand castle, plastering lumpy, wet handfuls of sand in all the wrong places. "No, no, you'll spoil it," said Jane. "Wait till we're finished, and you'll see how beautiful it is. You'll just love it."

It took at least an hour to finish the castle, because they kept thinking of new things to add to it. Finally Jane said they had waited long enough, and they could go swimming again. She called to Betsy: "Come and look at your lovely castle we made you."

But Betsy was squatting over a shapeless heap of sand, sticking broken shells into it every which way. "I don't want it," she said, without looking up. "I made a better one, all myself. And don't you touch it, either, or you'll spoil it."

So Jane and Don and Mike went swimming again, and the rising tide slowly melted the castle flat. They were all sun-soaked and water-soaked before it was time to get out and dry off and start for home. Jane stretched out flat on the warm sand and thought how nice and brown her arms and legs were getting. Don was brown, too, and Mike was all over freckles, except for his peeling nose. Betsy looked wonderful, all pink and tan, with her curls bleached out silvery-gold by the sun.

"Darn it!" Jane burst out. "Mike sure is lucky, getting to live here all the time! I wish we could stay here and really live here, go to school and everything. But no, we'll be right back in the middle of the city, with paved streets and traffic smells and no place to swim except that awful old pool. And Betsy will have croup again all winter, just the way she did last year."

"Oh, cheer up, for Pete's sake," said Don, flicking sand at her. "Let's just be healthy while we can. Mother's looking swell, too, have you noticed? I guess she really needed a vacation from that old library."

"Yes, and even Victoria is getting as fat as a pig," admitted Jane.

"Not on Miss Giddings's little feathered friends, I hope!" exclaimed Don. "If Miss Giddings ever catches Victoria with feathers in her teeth, the fur will fly."

"Whose fur?" asked Betsy anxiously.

Mike laughed. "Don's just talking," he told her. "Come on, I'll carry you piggy-back if you're too tired to walk."

They walked home, slowly and languidly. Mike took Betsy piggy-back, although Don prophesied gloomily that from now on Betsy would be too tired to walk anywhere.

"Mike is my friend," announced Betsy.

"Well, I like that!" said Don. "What am I?"

"You are only my brother," replied Betsy, holding on so tightly around Mike's neck that she nearly strangled him. Before they were halfway home, however, she loosened her grip and went sound asleep, with her head joggling on Mike's shoulder.

They cut through the alley and crossed the back

Mike took Betsy piggy-back.

lawn. An unfamiliar sound stopped them in their tracks: the wooden click of a croquet mallet hitting a ball. They all looked toward the side lawn.

"It must be sunstroke," groaned Don, clutching at his head. "I keep thinking I see this croquet game. And look who's playing!"

"Ssh! They'll hear you," warned Jane.

Mr. and Mrs. Baker, Miss Smith, and Mrs. Broome were indeed playing croquet. While Jane and Don and Mike goggled, Mr. Baker tapped the yellow ball through a wicket, so that it came to rest beside the red ball. Then he set his foot on the yellow ball and gave it a tremendous whack; the red ball skittered across the lawn to the edge of the street, and Mrs. Broome, who held the red mallet, groaned.

There was quite an audience. Miss Giddings, Mrs. Hand, and Mrs. Blessing sat under the big tree, and Mr. Blessing, in his wheel chair, completed the picture. The chair-sitters, thought Jane. Then she thought, that's funny, they don't look like chair-sitters any more. They look like people.

"And what do they care," muttered Don, with an accusing glance at Jane, "whether some brittle little children trip over their old wickets?"

Mike eased Betsy, still sleeping, onto her bed, and said he really had to go, and changed, and left. Don was hanging out the window, watching the croquet game. "Wow! Look at that Mrs. Broome sock that ball! You know something?" he asked, pulling his head in. "When we first came here, all the tenants looked just exactly alike, but they sure have changed. They're practically human."

"Nonsense, they haven't changed a bit," said Mother. "You've just been getting acquainted with them. And so have I. A fuse burned out while you were gone, and Mr. Baker got a new one from the tool shed and changed it for me. Then he asked if it was all right to use the croquet set."

"And I thought all any of them ever did was sit," marvelled Jane.

"They do a great deal more than sit," said Mother. "Professor Quincy writes articles for learned magazines, and Mrs. Hand is active in church work, and Mrs. Blessing was a trustee of the library and a member of the school board until her husband became so ill. And even Miss Giddings is a pillar of the local Audubon Society."

"Goodness, and is Mr. Baker something special, too?" asked Jane.

"He's a retired policeman from Jersey City," answered Mother.

"That's special enough for me," said Don thoughtfully, feeling in his pocket for his notebook full of clues. "Guess I'll try to get better acquainted with him."

"And Miss Smith isn't even retired," Mother went on. "She teaches in the High School. And Mrs. Broome is only living here until her son gets out of the Army. She's renting her own house until he returns with his family. She has a little granddaughter just Betsy's age, and she was telling me today that she has tried hard to get acquainted with Bets, but every time she speaks to her, somebody comes and snatches her away!"

"But you told me not to let her bother the tenants!" wailed Jane. "And I didn't."

"I know," admitted Mother. "And it seemed like a good idea at the time. But now I wonder if we weren't judging them all by Mrs. Pennypacker."

"Yes, what is *she* retired from?" demanded Don.

"Mrs. Pennypacker isn't retired," said Mother ruefully. "Her life's work has been minding other people's business, and she is just as active as ever!"

Big Wind

🐾 THE next morning the weather turned hot and sticky. There was no sun; there were no clouds, either. Just a depressing, muggy haze that brought out swarms of little biting insects. Betsy played for a while under the biscuit bush; then she came in, scratching and complaining, and hung around indoors underfoot.

Finally Don decided to brave the insects and mow the lawn. "It doesn't need it just awfully," he admitted, "but it'll be better for croquet if the grass is shorter."

"And then the croquet players will be so grateful to you that they'll invite you to play," suggested Jane.

"Something like that," said Don, grinning. "And I wouldn't expect to win, either. That Mrs. Broome sure swings a mean mallet. They all do."

He started the mower and got to work; but before he was halfway through with the side lawn, the motor spluttered and died. Jane went out and watched him doing all the things he had seen Mike do to the mower. He unscrewed this and that, and checked the air intake and the spark and the choke, and made sure there was gas in the tank.

"I guess I'll just have to wait till Mike comes," he admitted finally.

"I hope he comes soon then," said Jane. "Because it sure looks a lot worse half-mowed than it did before."

By lunch time, it was hotter and stickier than ever, without even a whisper of a breeze. Betsy was cross and fussy, and the minute she sat down at the table, she tipped over her milk.

"Now where is Victoria?" asked Mother, looking at the big puddle of milk on the floor. "That

cat is never around when she might be of some use
to us. I don't believe I've even seen her today."

"Neither have I," said Jane, thinking back.

"Maybe Miss Giddings caught her with feathers
in her teeth," said Don darkly. "I guess it's good-by
Victoria."

At this, Betsy began to cry, and Mother frowned
and shook her head at Don, and changed the sub-
ject. After Mother put Betsy in for her nap, Jane
and Don hung around a while longer, waiting for
Mike to show up. He didn't; so they finally went
swimming without him. The walk to the beach
seemed hotter and longer than usual, and they could
hardly wait to plunge into some cool, wet water.

But when they reached the ocean, it was rough
and sullen. Long gray waves were rolling in from the
horizon and crashing high up on the beach. "What
ails it today?" asked Jane. "I never saw it like this
before. And look how high the tide is, almost to the
top of the beach."

"Probably a storm way out at sea," said Don.

The breakers were too rough for swimming, but
Don and Jane got wet and cool, playing around in
the smother of foam that hissed up the sand. The
seagulls were noisier than usual, shrieking and cry-
ing over the crash of the breaking waves; and several

times long lines of pelicans flew overhead, following their leaders back inland. Jane and Don stayed until late afternoon, half expecting Mike to come running across the beach at any minute.

By the time they started back, a stiff breeze had sprung up, so they were still cool and damp when they reached town. On the main street, they saw men hammering away at the big wooden shutters over the plate glass shop windows.

"Oh, goody! They're opening up the stores that have been closed for the summer," exclaimed Jane.

"No, they're not either," said Don, after watching a minute. "They're boarding up the ones that were already open. I wonder why."

A high truck came around the corner and drove right up on the sidewalk. Its crew of men began unscrewing a big metal sign that said *Haberdashery* in neon letters. The back of the truck was already stacked with signs from other shops.

Don asked one of the men: "What's going on?"

"Where've you been, Buddy?" demanded the man. "Big wind coming. Hurricane. It's on the radio."

Don and Jane stared at him, open-mouthed. There was an old radio with a high curved top in Great-great-uncle John's apartment, but they hardly ever turned it on. It wasn't a very good one, and when they did manage to get the local station, or one of the Miami stations, they usually got a program in Spanish from Havana at the same time. They raced for home.

The first person they saw was Mike, hauling shutters out of the tool shed. "Hi!" he shouted. "Jane, your mother wants you, right away. Don, give me a hand with this stuff!"

Jane ran into the apartment. Mother had Great-great-uncle John's radio on full blast. An official voice was saying: "—disturbance in the Caribbean, which Navy planes have been watching for the last forty-eight hours, has picked up speed and headed for the Florida mainland. It is due to hit about halfway between Palm Beach and Miami around seven o'clock this evening. Hurricane warnings are up along the coast from Key West to Melbourne and as far inland as Lake Okeechobee. Residents of this area are asked to take the usual precautions."

"Goodness, what are the usual precautions?" shouted Jane above the noise of the radio.

Mother switched it off. "Oh, there you are. Jane, have you seen Betsy anywhere?"

"Why, no, we just got back from the beach, and Bets was asleep when we left."

"Oh, dear, she's wandered off somewhere. I wasn't paying too much attention, what with this hurricane business and all. Mike came by and offered to help, and I put him to work, and when I went to get Betsy, she was up and gone."

"I'll go look," said Jane. "She never goes far."

She combed the grounds thoroughly. The biscuit bush was empty, except for Betsy's collection of bright-colored trash; but Jane looked under all the other bushes, too. Sometimes, Betsy thought it was funny to sit quietly under a bush and listen to people calling her. Jane looked on the jungly side of the building, and into the tool shed. No Betsy.

Mike and Don were folding up the lawn chairs to put them away, and the wind caught the canvas and bellied it out like sails. Jane went up and down the street, asking everybody she saw whether they had noticed a little girl, about so high, with yellow curls. They all said no, they hadn't. Everybody was busy, boarding up windows and taking down awnings and moving in porch furniture; one man was walking around his yard with a long pole, knocking all the coconuts off his coconut palms. And everywhere was the sound of hammering, as people banged shutters into place over doors and windows.

Jane went back to the main street. Maybe Betsy

The canvas bellied out like sails.

had gone to watch the men on the truck take down the signs. But the truck was gone, and so were all the big hanging signs; the street looked strange and bare without them.

Jane looked far down the street, to where it turned into the road that led to the ocean. Surely Betsy had never tried to walk to the ocean all by herself! Jane remembered the ugly gray waves, crashing far up the beach and tumbling back again, sucking sand, shells, and seaweed into the ocean, to be pounded to bits by the next wave. A sudden gust of wind came tearing down the empty street, carrying fine stinging sand and torn newspapers with it.

She turned and ran for home, so fast it made her throat hurt. If Betsy hadn't turned up yet, she'd find a man, any man, with a car, and make him drive her out to the ocean, and—and—

The wind blew her into the front yard, where Don and Mike were hammering a solid wooden storm door into place, right over the front door. Professor Quincy was directing the job, shouting loudly above the rattling of the palm fronds. "We do this door first, faces southeast. That's where we'll get it first. Ought have shutters for all the windows on this side and I told McGregor so, but he knew better."

"A penny saved is a penny earned!" Jane heard Don shout back, as she kept on going around to the rear of the building.

And there was Betsy, sitting quietly on the back steps. Jane was so glad and so relieved that her knees felt all funny, and she sat down suddenly beside Betsy without really meaning to. Then she got angry.

"Where have you been?" she asked fiercely.

"Right here," said Betsy dreamily. "Visiting."

"Visiting who?"

"A lady. A nice lady." Betsy thought a minute, and added: "And she did so say *Come in!*"

Jane took her by the wrist and hauled her inside. "Which nice lady?" she demanded. "Show me the door."

Betsy pointed to number four.

"Not *Miss Giddings?*" asked Jane.

Betsy nodded.

"But Miss Giddings never, never says *Come in* to anybody," said Jane suspiciously. "Are you sure?"

Again Betsy nodded. "She said it to *me*," she remarked smugly.

Jane couldn't help asking: "What's it like in her apartment? I mean, is it just like ours?"

"Yes, except— *Oh!*" Betsy clapped her hand over

her mouth and looked at Jane with sparkling eyes. "It's a secret. I promised not to tell."

"Tell what?" coaxed Jane, but Betsy remained dumb. Jane took her into the apartment and turned her over to Mother, who breathed a sigh of relief.

"Now only Victoria is missing," said Mother. "And she's small enough to get in under a house or somewhere out of the storm. Let me see. Candles, flashlights, in case the electricity goes off. Canned goods, extra water, and a supply of mops and sponges, in case anything breaks and we have to mop. I think we have everything. Thank goodness the tenants are all hurricane veterans and are taking this in their stride. In fact, practically all of them have been in to reassure *me!* You might take another look around for Victoria. No, not you, Betsy. You sit right here, where I can keep an eye on you."

Jane went out again. It was much darker, and the gusts of wind were bringing heavy sudden splatters of rain. Professor Quincy was showing Don and Mike how to nail an enormous piece of plywood onto the back screen door.

"Can't nail this shut, like the front door," he shouted. "Might have to go in or out. That's right, never mind the nailholes, just wham her onto the frame. Makes the screen into a storm door. If we get the center here, second half will come from this direction."

"Is this the hurricane now?" shouted Jane.

"No, no. Fifty, sixty miles an hour. Hardly a full gale yet. Wait'll she hits a hundred. Can't hear yourself talk now, in forty minutes you won't be able to hear yourself think! Unless the whole shebang turns at the last minute and heads back to sea."

He looked disappointed at the very idea. Well, a hurricane made a nice change from the usual quiet life at 303 Oleander Drive, thought Jane.

Professor Quincy inspected the finished job, and said: "Well that's about it. Keep back from the windows—not likely to go, though; panes are too small. It's the big sheets of plate glass that just buckle, and —bang! Remember now, if we get the calm in the middle, don't go running out in it. And don't step in any puddles with broken wires in 'em. More fools get electrocuted than ever get brained by coconuts. Keep the radio on and do what the announcer tells you. Happy hurricane!"

With an amiable wave, he opened the back screen, now heavy with the added plywood, and disappeared into the building.

"What about the tool shed?" asked Mike suddenly. "If the door blows in. the roof'll go."

The rain was coming in earnest now, gray, blinding sheets of it that rattled like bullets on the side of the building, but Mike and Don ran out to nail up the tool shed door. Jane fought her way around the grounds once more, shrieking "Kitty, kitty!" above the roar of the wind and the rattling of the palm fronds.

She was soaked to the skin when she joined the boys at the back door. "Wow! Was that work!" exclaimed Don. "And am I hungry! I could eat a horse!" They all crowded, dripping, into number five.

"Why, Mike!" cried Mother in dismay. "I had no idea you were still here. You cut along for home now, just as fast as you can make it. Your parents will be simply frantic!"

Mike looked at her, and then down at the puddle at his feet. "I—I'd like to stay here, if I could," he mumbled.

"Why, you're welcome to stay here, Mike, you know that," said Mother warmly. "But you'll absolutely have to phone home and say where you are Quick, before the telephone lines blow down somewhere."

Mike continued to study the floor at his feet. "I

haven't got any phone," he said in a low voice. "In fact, I haven't got any home, either."

"But, Mike," said Mother, reasonably, "you must live *somewhere*."

Mike raised his eyes and looked at Mother. "Well, no. I don't. I mean—I live here, as much as I live anywhere." As Mother continued to look at him in bewilderment, he blurted out: "I've been sleeping in your tool shed and eating coconuts, except for what I ate here."

There was a moment's complete silence. Then Mother said, in a matter of fact voice: "Jane, change into dry things as fast as you can and help me get supper started. Don, take Mike across the hall, and the two of you get really dry. Lend Mike some clothes. We're all tired, and half starved, and the very first thing to do is to eat a good, big meal!"

At supper, Jane and Don tried hard to act just as usual, with the result that Jane chattered steadily about nothing at all, and they both laughed too much about things that weren't at all funny. But Betsy just stared silently at Mike all through the meal. When Mother took her off to bed, she stopped in the doorway and asked: "Don't you have any mother, Mike? Not any at all?"

"Not any at all," answered Mike.

"Oh, boy! Then you can stay up *all night!*" exclaimed Betsy enviously.

Everybody roared with laughter, even Mother. Even Mike. "Yes, I can," he admitted. "But it isn't much fun."

Jane washed the dishes, and Don and Mike dried. Outside, the wind howled steadily and the rain lashed the windows in solid sheets. The official voice on the radio droned on: "All Red Cross emergency crews, who have not already done so, are asked to report to their posts. Citizens will please cooperate by remaining indoors and off the streets. Police will enforce this regulation."

Mother reached over and snapped off the radio. "Do you want to tell us about it, Mike?" she asked gently.

Coconuts for Free

🏳 MIKE clasped and unclasped his hands in his lap, and kept his eyes on them. He began very slowly, and Jane got the idea that he was sorting things over in his head, deciding what to say and what not to say.

"Well, uh. I've been going to this school in Pennsylvania. The Industrial Home School, it's called. It isn't a reform school, or anything like that," he assured Mother anxiously. "It's just a school that boys live at that haven't got any place else to live. Anyway, it isn't so bad. We do all sorts of shop work, and there's a farm along with it, and we work on that, too, and the teachers are tough, but fair. There's a good ball field, and a swimming pool. And I *did* pass my Junior Lifesaving last year," he added, looking at Mother.

"Well, in the summers, the school closes for a couple of months, and most of the kids go off and live around, with different families. I think the county pays 'em board money for us. Well, this summer I got a really mean family to live with."

Jane looked at Mother and Don, and thought of Betsy, asleep in the next room, and tried to imagine what it would be like to be dumped down on a strange family, but she couldn't.

Mike went on: "They lived out of town a ways, and had five or six acres of truck garden and a boy about my age. The man was pretty strict and I sure had to work my head off, but he made his own boy work just as hard, so I didn't mind. But his wife— Gee, I don't hardly know how to explain it!" he burst out. "She was just *after* me, all the time, whatever I did. Or didn't do. It got so I was almost afraid to breathe, for fear she'd bawl me out for using too much air. And she watched every mouthful I ate, like it almost killed her to waste the food on me. And she kept telling Joey, that was the boy, to keep away from me so he wouldn't pick up bad habits. Well, it was only for the summer, and I thought I could stick it out, but after about a month of it, I just quit. I took a couple of dollars I'd been saving up, and said I was going to spray lima beans in a field right beside the highway. I got a hitch into town right away, and I knew nobody'd miss me till suppertime. And by suppertime, I was somewhere down in Maryland, and heading south."

"I'm surprised that drivers would pick up a boy your age and take you so far," said Mother. "Where in the world did they think you were going?"

"Well, I always thought up something to tell 'em," said Mike, squirming uncomfortably. "Maybe it wasn't always exactly true, but it wasn't really lies, either. I never asked for long hitches, because somebody might get the idea I was running away and notify the police. What I'd do, I'd find out the name of the next big town—twenty, thirty miles up the road—and then I'd ask for a ride that far, like I lived there and was on my way home. It takes longer that way, but I wasn't in any hurry, once I got out of Pennsylvania."

"Why did you pick out Florida to come to?" asked Don with interest.

"Oh, lots of reasons. If I was going to get in trouble for running away, I figured I might as well see the country first. Then, I knew I'd have to eat, and we studied about Florida at school. Coconuts growing wild, and all you have to is pick 'em up off the ground and bust 'em open and eat 'em. And it's true, too." Mike made an awful face. "But, oh brother, am I sick of coconuts!"

They all laughed, and Jane asked: "Goodness, Mike, how long have you been living on coconuts, anyway?"

"Well, I don't know. Remember when I caught your cat? Well, that was the day I got here. I was just coming in to see if you wanted your lawn mowed, and I picked up the cat and came in with you, and, boy, it was pretty confused in here! The manager was missing, and Miss Giddings was talking, and I couldn't get a word in edgewise to ask about the lawn, so I left. Remember that day?"

"I certainly do!" replied Mother, with feeling. "Then what did you do?"

"Well, I tried a few more places, then I came back and slept in your tool shed. I'd already noticed it.

Next day I went all over, looking for jobs, but there weren't any, so I came back to see about your lawn again, but there was a boy already mowing it. I guess you know the rest," he finished.

"Did you take the mysterious missing can of beans?" asked Don, grinning.

"Yes, I did." Mike looked awfully upset. "They'd just been sitting on the shelf, and sitting on it, and I thought maybe you didn't like beans. I'd already hidden it in the tool shed when you missed it, and I couldn't figure out any way to put it back. Well, so I ate the beans, then I went to put the can in the big trash can, but it was empty, so I knew you'd see it first thing. So I buried it in somebody's trash basket, early, but you found it anyway. But, honest and truly, that's the only single thing I ever did take, and I felt perfectly awful about it." Mike looked desperately at Mother.

"Heavens, Mike, you were welcome to all the beans you could eat! But why in the world didn't you tell us all this before?"

Mike was silent for some time before he answered. Suddenly Jane was aware of the storm again. The wind was still howling, but now the sound rose occasionally to a high-pitched shriek that hurt her ears.

Something was slap, slapping against the building just outside, one of the palm trees, probably. It
sounded like whips cracking. Then the wind quieted
for an instant, and she could just hear the long mourn-
ful toot-toot of a train going through town. Goodness, what if you had to get off a train right in the
middle of a hurricane?

"Well, I liked it here," said Mike gruffly. "Everybody was nice to me, and besides I could see I could
be a real help around the place. But if I said anything—about how I ran away and all— Well, I was
scared that I would just get shipped back right away."
He looked sidewise at Mother as he said this.

Jane and Don looked at Mother, too, anxiously;
but Mother was frowning down at her lap.

"Oh, Mother!" cried Jane accusingly. "You
wouldn't send him back to those awful people,
would you? *Would* you, Mother?"

"This sort of thing is always more complicated
than it seems to children," said Mother slowly, in a
troubled voice. "The people he was staying with must
have notified the school. And if the school is responsible for him, they must have notified the police. You
see, *somebody* has to be responsible for him until he's
old enough to earn a living."

"Then we'll adopt him, and we can be responsible for him!" cried Jane enthusiastically. "How about that?"

"Hot diggity!" shouted Don. "That's the most sensible idea you ever had. How about it, Mother?"

"That's complicated, too," said Mother seriously. "There are all sorts of laws about it. For instance, if either of his parents is living—"

Suddenly the door popped open and Miss Giddings simply flew into the room. "Oh dear, I do hate to bother you," she gasped, wringing her hands, "but please come quick! One of my windows has broken —something blew against it—and water is simply pouring in!"

Mike and Don ran for the hammer, nails, and boards that they had brought in, for just such an emergency.

"And that's not the worst of it," Miss Giddings went on distractedly. "Poor Chico is so upset I can't get near him, and goodness knows what he'll do next. Wait, boys! Wait! I'll go with you."

She trotted out and led Don and Mike into her apartment. Mother and Jane grabbed up rags, and followed.

There was a small pane broken out of an upper

sash, and wind and rain were whistling through, making a noisy, wet mess of the room. The boys set to work quickly, boarding up the broken window, and Mother started mopping up the puddles on the rug.

Above the noise of the storm and the boys' hammering, Jane heard a shattering crash in Miss Giddings's kitchen. Another window, she thought, and ran into the kitchen; but the window in there was undamaged. Then she saw a tiny dark figure, huddled in the dish cupboard. Why, it was a little monkey, chattering and shivering. It held a saucer in its tiny black hands.

"Chico!" cried Miss Giddings despairingly. "Put it down!"

Chico hurled the saucer onto the floor, where it smashed into a dozen pieces.

"What in the world?" exclaimed Mother, appearing in the doorway.

"Oh dear, a storm always upsets him," moaned Miss Giddings. "He was very restless, even before the window broke, and then— No, no! Chico, please!"

But Chico, chattering wildly, tossed a cream pitcher after the saucer. Mike and Don crowded into the kitchen to see what was going on.

Chico hurled the saucer.

Mother firmly herded everybody out of the room. "Too many people," she said. "No wonder the poor little thing is upset."

"Oh, dear Mrs. Sanders, you are so understanding!" cried Miss Giddings. "I am so sorry you had to see Chico like this. He has never been in the least destructive— Except the dishes, and they are my own," she added hastily, as there was another crash from the kitchen. "You can ask your little girl about him—not this one, the very little one, with the curls. She was in here only this afternoon, and Chico loved her. He cuddled right down in her lap, and she played with him so sweetly."

"Did you really ask Betsy in?" blurted Jane. "We thought— I mean, we've told her over and over again to keep out of people's apartments."

"Yes, indeed. She was looking for her lost kitty. I cannot say that I am fond of cats, ordinarily, but I couldn't help thinking how I would feel if my Chico were lost. Yes, I asked her in and gave her a cooky, and Chico took to her immediately, although he is not at all used to strangers. I don't, as a rule, encourage visitors." Miss Giddings looked anxiously at Mother. "The late Mr. McGregor was very firm about pets in the apartments—very firm. So I have always thought it best to say nothing, to anybody, about Chico."

Mother patted Miss Giddings on the shoulder. "That's all right. As long as I keep the apartment, you are quite welcome to have Chico here."

"Oh, Mrs. Sanders! I cannot tell you what this means to me. Chico is all the family I have, and this apartment is all the home I have. I have been so worried for fear I would have to give up one or the other. Why, I can get a little leash, and take him right out on the lawn with me!"

Miss Giddings was so grateful that it was almost embarrassing, and Jane was glad when the boys finished with the window and they could all leave.

They made a tour of inspection before going back to number five. A good deal of water was being driven in under the boarded-up front door, so they mopped up, and then stuffed rags into the crack under the door. Mrs. Pennypacker opened her door and complained that her ceiling was leaking.

"Put a pan under it," suggested Mother.

"I already have!" snapped Mrs. Pennypacker, and slammed the door.

"Gee, does she expect us to run right out and patch the roof?" asked Don.

The back door was on the side away from the wind, so they opened it cautiously and peered out. They could just see the electric and phone wires over their heads snap-snapping crazily, like jump ropes; one of them was giving off fizzy blue sparks. They could hear a loud banging noise above the other noises, which Don thought must be the door of the tool shed. He and Mike wanted to go out and investigate it, but Mother said they would do no such thing.

Back in number five, Don took out his notebook and looked at it gloomily. "Another good clue gone glimmering," he said. "Mr. Brundage is not sleeping on our awnings and swiping beans, and Miss Giddings is not a kleptomaniac. Doggone, I haven't got hardly any clues left!"

"What in the world are you talking about?" demanded Mother.

"Oh, just some things I jotted down," he mumbled. He turned on the radio and got a lot of crackling static, and a voice saying: "—report sustained winds of eighty-five miles an hour and gusts up to a hundred and twenty-five miles an hour. Stay tuned to this station for the next weather re—"

The radio stopped dead. The lights flickered and went out. They all bumped into each other in the dark, looking for the candles and getting them lighted.

Suddenly Jane yawned. Mike and Don started yawn-
ing, and couldn't stop. They all protested that they
weren't sleepy, not a bit, but Mother bundled them
off to bed, just the same.

She sent Don and Mike across the hall to number
six. "Just take off your shoes and sleep in your
clothes," she told them. "If there's an emergency and
I need you, I may need you in a hurry. Jane can sleep
with Betsy, and I'll just lie down on the sofa here,
because this is where people will expect to find me if
they need me."

Jane, too, took off only her shoes, and lay down
next to Betsy in the bedroom. She could see Mother's
candle glimmering in the next room, and she lay
awake, listening to the storm.

Poor Victoria, out in all this weather. Still, nobody
took care of birds and squirrels in a hurricane, and
they got along all right. At least, Mike wasn't out in
it, and that was the main thing. Maybe Mother could
fix it, somehow, so that he didn't have to go back to
those awful people. Mother blew out her candle, and
Jane shoved Betsy over a little farther in the bed, and
closed her eyes.

Mr. Brundage Comes

✹ Somebody was knocking on the door of the apartment, knocking so loudly that it could be heard over the roar and rattle of the storm, knocking so loudly that it woke Jane up. She sat up in bed and called, "Mother!"

"I hear it," replied Mother. She turned her flashlight on the doorway, and called: "Come in!"

The door opened, and a man stood there. He was dripping wet and exhausted looking, and he had one arm in a sling. He blinked at the flashlight and said: "Hello. Is this apartment occupied?"

"What do you want?" asked Mother sharply.

Jane leaned forward to hear his reply, but what he said took her by surprise. "Maybe this is your cat. It came in with me just now."

Mother turned the flashlight onto the floor at his feet, and there was Victoria, her fur flat and wet, and her green eyes gleaming in the light. "Why, Victoria!" said Mother. "Oh, goodness, she's got a mouse in her mouth!"

Victoria streaked in, right through the bedroom door, and jumped up beside Jane. "*Eeek!*" squealed Jane. "It's a rat! No, it isn't. It's a *kitten!*"

And so it was. Victoria stood over it, purring proudly and licking the poor drenched little thing. At first Jane thought it was dead; then it opened its tiny pink mouth and squeaked. Victoria promptly jumped off the bed and ran back to the door, making little anxious noises in her throat.

"Oh, Mother!" cried Jane, leaping out of bed. "She's got some more, some place, and she wants me to come with her. Oh, Mother, let me have the flashlight!"

"In this weather!" exclaimed Mother. "It isn't safe."

"I'll go with her," offered the strange man, unexpectedly. "I can't get any wetter."

"Oh, dear," said Mother distractedly. "Wait, Jane. Put on my raincoat and button it up. I'll wear this one."

Then they all three followed Victoria out the back door. The wind shrieked, the rain split the flashlight beam into dancing splinters, and the water was ankle-deep on the back lawn. Victoria led them straight to the tool shed. The tool shed door leaned inward at a drunken angle, hanging by one hinge. Victoria disappeared into the blackness inside.

"I'll get them!" shouted Jane. "I know my way around in there." She took the flashlight from Mother and went in. And in the farthest corner, beside the paint cans in the old sink, lay two more kittens on a pile of greasy rags. Jane gathered them up, while Victoria pranced anxiously around her ankles.

Then they all fought their way back to the shelter of the building, with Victoria running ahead.

"And now," said Mother to the man, as they stood dripping and breathless in number five apartment again, "who are you?"

"I am the manager here," he replied. "At least, I was. I suppose the new owner couldn't wait for me to come back, and hired you."

"I am the new owner," said Mother. "So you're Mr. Brundage. I must say a great many people have been wondering what had become of you."

"Didn't you get my letter?" asked Mr. Brundage in a surprised voice. "Mr. McGregor gave me your name and address while he was in the hospital. I wrote to you the day I left here, explaining all about it."

"The letter would have arrived in Philadelphia after I reached here. It must be there still. I'm afraid I didn't leave any forwarding address, as I only expected to be here a few days. But, goodness, we don't have to stand here dripping while we talk. Take off that raincoat, Jane, and bring Victoria and the kittens into the kitchen. Mr. Brundage, you'll find your things still in the bedroom. Here, take a candle, and don't worry about Betsy. Nothing wakes her up. Oh, dear, I do believe this is your raincoat I'm wearing! I just grabbed it out of the closet."

Mother got some coffee started on the stove; luckily the gas hadn't been turned off with the electricity. Jane fixed a grocery carton in a dark corner for the kittens, and fed Victoria a large meal under the sink. Then she sat very quietly beside the kittens, hugging her knees, while Mother and Mr. Brundage had sandwiches and coffee in the kitchen by candlelight.

The sandwiches looked delicious and Jane was

famished, but she didn't dare mention it, for fear Mother would remember to send her back to bed. Wouldn't the boys be furious if they knew what they were sleeping through! New kittens, and the mysterious missing Mr. Brundage!

Not that he was missing any more, and he didn't look especially mysterious, either, now that he had changed into dry clothes. Just rather tired and sad, Jane thought. Anyway, she was glad that he had come back in the middle of a hurricane, so that Mrs. Pennypacker couldn't pounce right on him and start in about her poor dear mother's ruby.

Mother hadn't mentioned Mrs. Pennypacker's ruby clip. She was only asking him how he had happened to go to work for Great-great-uncle John.

"It was just luck that I walked in, looking for a job, at the very time he got too sick to take care of the place himself," explained Mr. Brundage. "I'm not really a handyman. I'm a machinist. But I haven't been in very good health lately. In and out of hospitals for a couple of years, and that can really eat up your savings. Finally the doctors said I had to get some other kind of work, something in a warmer climate that would keep me outdoors a good deal. Actually, I think McGregor took me on because I offered to work for next to nothing, in return for—"

Mr. Brundage broke off and took another sip of coffee. "I wish you had gotten my letter," he said slowly. "It explained everything, much better than I can do now, talking. I suppose you know that your uncle wasn't particularly fond of children?"

"I don't believe he was," replied Mother, looking mystified.

"But he was fond of saving money wherever he could," went on Mr. Brundage, with a little smile, "so he hired me, even though it meant having a child in the building."

"A child?" asked Mother, looking around as though Mr. Brundage might have left a baby in a corner.

"Yes. His mother died when he was little, and it's hard for a man, alone, to raise a kid the right way. Factory towns, where I could find the best-paying jobs, were pretty tough places and no good for a boy running wild all day. Then I was in the hospital, not earning anything. So I had to—well, to put him into a sort of public institution, so I haven't even seen much of him for a couple of years. But this arrangement seemed ideal. I would be working right where I lived, and I could have him with me, and I really looked this town over and decided it would be a nice little place for a boy to grow up in."

"I see," said Mother sympathetically. "So you went up north to get him?"

"Not exactly. I couldn't get him yet, because I hadn't made any arrangements with you. But I had to go, just the same, because he ran away from some people he was staying with. I saw them, and I can't say I blame him. But he had been missing nearly a week before I was notified. Then it took me a while to pick up his tracks. He'd been hitchhiking, and heading south, so I knew he was headed right here. He had this address, you see, because I'd been writing to him. *This* didn't help, either." Mr. Brundage touched the sling on his arm. "My money was running low, so I picked up a ride on a truck, and it overturned in South Carolina, and I had to stop and get my arm set. I came on by train, as soon as I could, and it took me an hour to get across town. Had to argue with policemen and storm wardens on every corner."

By this time, Jane was just about to burst with excitement, and Mother sounded pretty excited, too, as she asked: "What's your son's name?"

"Michael. Has he been here, asking for me?" said Mr. Brundage eagerly.

"Well, there's been a boy around, named Mike, but he hasn't said anything about you."

Mr. Brundage's face fell. "It must be some other boy. If Mike came all the way to Florida to find me, why, the first thing he'd do would be to ask for me right here."

"I bet I know why he didn't!" Jane burst out.

"I thought you were in bed," said Mother. "Do you know what time it is?"

"Why didn't he?" asked Mr. Brundage.

"Well, he ran away from some mean people on a truck farm, and he's maybe twelve or thirteen and he has freckles, and we like him a lot," began Jane, all in one breath.

"That *must* be Mike!" cried Mr. Brundage. "But why didn't he say who he was and ask for me?"

"I think maybe—well, the very minute he got here, everybody was saying you had gone away and nobody knew where, and then Mrs. Pennypackeɪ made a big noise about her ruby clip being missing and said you weren't coming back. Anyway, even if Mike didn't think—" Jane stopped in confusion.

"That I stole it," finished Mr. Brundage.

"Oh, I'm sure he never thought *that*, but the thing is, he didn't know *what* to think," explained Jane. "He probably knew all the time you'd gone to look for him and you'd be back, but he thought that if he said who he was, people would ask where he came from, and then they'd ship him right back there to that awful place. So I guess he just decided to hang around till you got back, only it took you a lot longer than he thought it would."

"Poor kid," said Mr. Brundage. "Well, it's something to know you've seen him and he isn't sick or anything. As soon as this weather lets up a bit, I'll go look for him."

Jane looked at Mother and Mother looked at Jane. Then Mother said cautiously: "Don't be too disappointed if it isn't the right boy. But if it is, he's in the apartment across the hall, asleep."

"*What!*" Mr. Brundage leaped to his feet. "Which apartment?"

Mother took the flashlight and led the way. Both boys, fully dressed, were sprawled on Great-great-uncle John's bed. Mike was lying on his back with one arm across Don's chest. Mother played the flash on his face, and he mumbled something in his sleep and rolled over.

"Yes. This is Mike," whispered Mr. Brundage, leaning over the bed.

Mother touched him on the shoulder and beckoned him out of the room. "Let him sleep," she said. "He's had a hard day."

Back in number five, Mr. Brundage looked like a

Both boys, fully dressed, were sprawled on the bed.

different person. He stood up straighter, and Jane could see why some of the tenants had described him as quite a young man.

"Why, you've taken him in without knowing who he was or anything about him," he said to Mother. "I can't even begin to thank you for it. But I'll be glad to work here, for nothing, if I can keep the job and the apartment. I'm sure I could find a part-time job somewhere else that would pay for our food."

"It's too late to talk business tonight," said Mother, smiling. "The sofa over in number six is made up to sleep on, so why don't you just turn in over there? That way, I'm sure you'll see Mike the minute he wakes up in the morning."

"Thank you," said Mr. Brundage. "And good night."

"Good night," said Mother.

"Good night," said Jane.

"For goodness sakes, are you still up, young lady?" exclaimed Mother. "You march right in there to bed."

Jane lay awake until Mother blew the candle out again. "Mother!" she called softly. "You will let him stay, and keep Mike here, won't you?"

"I don't know," replied Mother, in a troubled

voice. "When he thinks it over, he may not want to stay. There's still that miserable ruby clip to be accounted for."

"Oh, but, *Mother!* You don't think he took it, or Mike, either?"

"No, but it doesn't matter what I think. If it doesn't turn up, you know what Mrs. Pennypacker will think, and what she will say. And she will go right on saying it. Of course, she won't be able to prove that he took it, but how can he prove that he didn't? It's likely to be very unpleasant. Now go to sleep."

Jane closed her eyes obediently, but something was keeping her awake. Something more than excitement; and it took her a while to figure out what it was. It was the silence! The center of the hurricane must be passing over. Jane's ears were so used to the tremendous smother of noise outside that the silence seemed to echo in her head. She twisted and turned, trying to get comfortable, weighted down by the stillness. It was so still that she could hear the drip, drip of water from the leaves, right through the closed windows. It was so still that she could hear the tiny squeak of a new kitten, all the way from the kitchen, and Victoria's reassuring *prrraow.* Then, with a roar that rattled all the windows, the second half of the hurricane hit. The wind bellowed, the rain battered against the building, and Jane rolled over and went to sleep.

Mrs. Pennypacker Goes

✎ WHEN Jane woke up in the morning, for one bewildered moment she couldn't think where she was and why she had all her clothes on. Someone had opened the bedroom window; the sun was simply blazing outside and the sky was a bright dazzling blue and there was just enough breeze to flick the edge of the window curtain. Betsy's side of the bed was empty and there was a cheerful confusion of voices in the kitchen.

Jane rubbed her eyes, straightened her rumpled

shirt, and walked into the kitchen barefoot. Betsy was sitting on the floor beside the kitten box, eating a piece of buttered toast and beaming at the kittens as proudly as though she had invented them herself. Everybody else was crowded in at the little kitchen table.

Mike was sitting next to his father, and he looked like a brand new Mike. The Mike Jane knew had a wary, watchful look on his face and hardly ever said anything except in answer to a question. This Mike wore a big wide grin that stayed on even while he chewed. Even while he talked. And he was talking steadily.

"The toughest thing," he was saying cheerfully, "was keeping away from the place enough of the time so that you all wouldn't start wondering, Gosh, doesn't he have any place *else* to live? Man, I sure walked all over this town, and up and down the beach for miles, just staying out of sight. And I never got enough sleep, because I was scared to turn in till all the lights in the place went out, and I had to get up awful early so nobody would come out and catch me in the tool shed. And the reason I took that can of beans was because you said they were Mr. Brundage's beans, and I thought, Gee, if I can't eat my own father's beans, what can I eat?"

His father interrupted him. "I hope the barbershop is open today," he said, looking at Mike's hair.

Mike brushed the hair back out of his eyes and exposed a dazzling white forehead above his tanned and freckled face.

Don whistled. "Oh, brother, are you ever going to get a fierce sunburn after you have a haircut! The back of your neck, too."

"The detecting business must be looking up," observed Jane, reaching for a piece of toast. "I see you've found Mr. Brundage already."

"The trouble with the detecting business," growled Don, "is that nobody tells anybody the truth."

"Everything I told you was the truth," replied Mike amiably.

"Huh, it sure wasn't the whole truth."

"Look, if everybody went around telling the whole truth the whole time, what would there be for the detectives to detect? You better get busy and detect Mrs. Pennypacker's ruby clip, or she'll go on saying that Dad took it."

"Let her find it herself, if she wants it so bad," grunted Don. "I'm out of the detecting business as of right now."

After breakfast, they left the dirty dishes right on the table. Betsy couldn't tear herself away from the kitten box, but everybody else went out the back door to look around. Nothing was the same, after the storm.

All along the street the light poles leaned over at different angles, trailing broken wires, but already there were men with trucks, repairing the damage. Half a dozen palms were down, flat on the ground, with their roots in the air. For such tall trees, the roots were ridiculously small; they looked like old kitchen mops. A huge branch had snapped off the old live oak and lay sprawled half across the lawn, along with a section of somebody's picket fence, a sodden straw hat, part of an awning with a twisted frame, and about two-thirds of a billboard with the left side of a beautiful lady and the words, *Drink Coc,* painted on it. And all over everything was a litter of coconut fronds, twigs, leaves and petals. The trees and bushes were just clumps of naked stems and branches, whipped bare by the wind.

"Oh dear, look at Betsy's poor biscuit bush!" cried Jane. "All her precious junk." Betsy's bedraggled collection was plastered up against the base of the building, embedded in a drift of sand and rubbish. Jane crawled under the bare bushes on her hands and knees and began rescuing what she could.

Don went off with Mike and Mr. Brundage to get

tools and unbar the front door; Jane saw them carrying the ramp around the building, in case Mr. Blessing wanted to come out and view the damage, too.
Other tenants were already coming out the back door
and scattering around the grounds, looking happily
up at the clear sky and reminiscing about past hurricanes with the air of experts.

"Absolutely nothing compared to the '47 blow,"
Miss Smith was saying. "Three feet of water in the
middle of town and the yacht basin overflowed and
there were yachts all over the A and P parking lot."

"I remember a typhoon once, in the China Sea,"
said Mrs. Hand in her gentle voice. "Little junks piled
up all along the beach, and the poor fishermen and
their families—those boats were their homes and
their livelihood both—"

"Ah, but you should have been here for the Big
Blow of '26!" exclaimed Mrs. Broome. "There wasn't
a single house undamaged in town, and I don't know
how many just blew away and were never seen again.
We had just moved here from Chicago, and my
husband and I were sitting at a window on the lee
side of the house, watching things blow by, and my
husband said: 'There goes another roof!' Then we
looked up, and it was our own roof."

Jane crawled along the side of the building, pick-

ing up Betsy's shells and empty perfume bottles and
tin badges, the kind you find in cereal boxes, and the
little plastic toys that sometimes come out of a chewing gum machine when you put a penny in. What a
magpie the child was! And a piece of shiny ten-cent-
store jewelry. Jane picked up the glittering thing and
brushed it off on her shirt front.

Splinters of blueish light sparkled from the white
stones around the edge, and the red stone in the
middle glowed warmly without sparkling. Jane didn't
even have to turn it over and make sure that there
was a gold spring clip on the back. It didn't matter
that she had never seen a real ruby in her whole life,
this thing looked so exactly the way she had always
known a ruby would look.

Jane sat back on her heels. Now where in the world
had Betsy picked it up? Could Mrs. Pennypacker
have dropped it outdoors somewhere, and Betsy, with
her sharp eyes—? Surely she had never taken it from
Mrs. Pennypacker's apartment! Then Jane had a sudden vision of Mrs. Pennypacker in the doorway with
Betsy, and Betsy saying, *I had to get my shoes.* Jane's
heart sank. Betsy would never, never take anything
out of a box, or off a table, Jane was certain of that;
but any shiny object on the floor was simply treasure-
trove to her.

Jane picked up the glittering thing.

And now there was the unpleasant business of returning this thing to Mrs. Pennypacker, who would certainly call poor little Betsy a thief or worse. Well, Mother would know what to do. Jane put the ruby clip in the pocket of her shorts and backed out from under the bushes.

She found Mother near the front door, standing beside Mr. Blessing's wheel chair and deep in conversation with Mrs. Blessing. Jane hung around, waiting for a chance to speak to her alone. Mr. Brundage was examining the ramp, while Mike and Don proudly showed him how they had fixed it to fit over the steps.

Miss Giddings came out the door, with Chico on an improvised leash, made of a belt and a ribbon tied together. She walked down the steps beside the ramp, looked up at the sky, and exclaimed: "What a glorious morning! Simply glorious! It just goes to show."

Next came Mrs. Pennypacker, looking for Mother. She interrupted Mother's conversation with Mrs. Blessing. "Something must be done about the roof! Immediately. It leaked bucketfuls, all night." Suddenly she caught sight of Chico. "Eeeeek!" she screeched. "What's that?"

Chico was not accustomed to being screeched at. He darted out the full length of his leash and made a quick grab for the flounce on the bottom of Mrs. Pennypacker's skirt, and it ripped loose with a loud tearing noise. Miss Giddings scolded and pulled on the leash; Chico chattered and pulled on the flounce; and just as the whole thing came off in Chico's little hands, Betsy burst out the front door, shouting at the top of her lungs: "Guess what, everybody! *Kittens*, and all brand new!" She slid down the ramp, bumped into Mrs. Pennypacker at the bottom, and dashed off around the building, still yelling: "Kittens! Three kittens!"

Mrs. Pennypacker, ignoring Miss Giddings's apologies, shouted at Mother: "This place is no better than a madhouse! I am giving you my notice! I am leaving. But you haven't heard the last of me. What about my poor dear mother's—"

She stopped short. She pointed a quivering finger at Mr. Brundage, who was standing quietly by, with a hammer in his hand. "There he is!" she gasped. "There's the man who stole it! Do something, don't let him get away, call the police!"

Jane forgot that she was going to have a quiet talk with Mother. She just stepped up to Mrs. Pennypacker and waved the ruby clip right under her nose. Mrs. Pennypacker snatched it from her and examined it suspiciously. "Hah!" she snorted. "So he decided to bring it back." And she marched into the building without a backward glance.

"He didn't take it!" Jane called after her, but the screen door slammed on the words, drowning them out.

Don and Mike pounced on her with questions, but it was to Mother that Jane explained miserably: "The biscuit bush. In with all the rest of Betsy's junk. I suppose it's been there all this time. Oh, Mother, you *know* she didn't have any idea—"

"And Mrs. Pennypacker still thinks Dad took it!" exclaimed Mike. "The awful old—"

"Stinker," suggested Don helpfully.

"I'll tell her where we found it before she goes," said Mother.

"No. Don't," said Mr. Brundage firmly. "You can't tell a person like that anything. If she's really going, just let her go."

And go she did, the very next morning, which was just as soon as she could get a truck to come and take her things away.

But even Mrs. Pennypacker's departure seemed un-important, compared to Mother's big news. Mother had decided not to sell the building, but to keep it, and to stay here and live in it.

Jane was wild with excitement. She hugged Mother and she hugged Betsy, and she would have hugged Don and Mike, too, except that she knew they wouldn't speak to her for a week if she did. She hardly heard Mother's explanation about how none of the people who were interested in buying the prop-erty intended to keep the building as it was. They all planned to remodel it, or tear it down and build some-thing else; and the first thing they all planned to do was to tell the tenants to leave.

"I've been hoping to see some way to keep the place for some time," Mother explained. "But nearly all the rent money for months and months will have to go for taxes, and after that there are some really expensive repairs that must be made if the place isn't to tumble down around our ears. I just couldn't see what we would do for living expenses if I gave up my job. But with my new job at the Palm Glade library—"

"What about the Palm Glade library?" asked Jane.

"For goodness sake, Jane, quit leaping around the

room, and *listen*. Mrs. Blessing knows all about the library. She was a trustee for years, and when she found out the other day that I was a librarian, she seemed quite excited, although I couldn't imagine why. So now the trustees have offered me the librarian's job. Of course, I haven't even seen the place yet—"

"Oh, it's darling," exclaimed Jane. "You'll just love it, but it's closed for the summer now."

"No, it's closed because the librarian got married and moved away. So we'll just move into Mrs. Pennypacker's apartment. It's a really big one, with two enormous bedrooms. I can't imagine why she needed the biggest one in the building."

"Because *she* was the biggest one in the building," Don whispered to Mike, but he made sure Mother couldn't hear him.

"And Mike and his father will live in number five, of course, and a teacher friend of Miss Smith's is just waiting to rent number six. Oh, and Mrs. Broome has told me about a fine nursery school near here, so Jane won't have to spend all her time baby-sitting. And the library's open only three days a week, so I won't have to spend all *my* time—"

Mother paused for breath. "There's so much to

do!" she exclaimed. "We must send for our things and get really settled here before school starts. And you will have to get registered for school in a few days, and Mike, too. Miss Smith has offered to go with you and show you what to do. Heavens, I hardly know what to do first!"

"*I* know what to do first," said Jane suddenly. "In all the time we've been here, I don't believe you've been to the ocean even once."

"That's right," admitted Mother. "I haven't."

"Then I think we should all get our bathing suits and go swimming. All in favor say *Aye!*"

"*Aye!*" shouted Don and Mike.

"*Aye!*" shouted Betsy. "What does aye mean?"

"All right," said Mother, laughing. "Just this once, to celebrate. But there's something I must attend to first. Get me a hammer and a screwdriver, will you?"

"If it's something to repair, I'll do it," said Mr. Brundage.

"No, this is something I have been meaning to do for a long time, and I want to do it myself."

Mother carried the tools out to the front door. Then, while Mr. Brundage and Jane and Don and Mike and Betsy and Victoria all stood and watched, Mother removed the signs that said:

NO CHILDREN. NO PETS.

and handed them to Mr. Brundage.

"Just throw these in the trash, will you?" she asked. "And now, we'll all go swimming."

A NOTE ON THE TYPE

THE TEXT of this book is set in ELECTRA, a Linotype face designed by W. A. Dwiggins. This face cannot be classified as either "modern" or "old-style." It is not based on any historical model, nor does it echo any particular period or style. It avoids the extreme contrast between "thick" and "thin" elements that mark most "modern" faces, and attempts to give a feeling of fluidity, power, and speed.